J Fic
Christopher, John.
New found land.

Dutton, 1983
135 p. ;

New Found Land

Books by John Christopher

Empty World

Fireball
and
New Found Land

THE TRIPODS TRILOGY
The White Mountains
The City of Gold and Lead
The Pool of Fire

THE SWORD TRILOGY
The Prince in Waiting
Beyond the Burning Lands
The Sword of the Spirits

The Lotus Caves
The Guardians
Dom and Va
Wild Jack

New Found Land

by John Christopher

E. P. Dutton New York

First published in the U.S.A. 1983 by E. P. Dutton, Inc.,
2 Park Avenue, New York, New York 10016

Library of Congress Cataloging in Publication Data

Christopher, John.
New found land.

Summary: Encountering a fireball which turns out to be a crossing point between their world and another one on a different probability track, two boys, one English and one American, face Indians, Vikings and Aztecs in their attempts to reach California. Sequel to Fireball.
[1. Space and time—Fiction.] I. Title.
PZ7.C457Ne 1983 [Fic] 82-18354
ISBN 0-525-44049-6

Editor: Ann Durell

Printed in the U.S.A. First Edition
10 9 8 7 6 5 4 3 2 1

to Charlotte de Putron
with love

1

THERE WERE SEVERAL minor falls of snow before the big one. It started quietly enough, with a few flecks floating down from a steel-grey sky, dissolving as they touched the ground. This was early afternoon, and the gentle fall continued until dark. They brought in logs for the fire, ate their evening meal by lamplight, and afterwards played a Roman game with dice and counters.

Next morning the snow was still falling, but faster and more thickly, and it was more than a foot deep against the door. They looked at a white world, and when they went outside their voices were strange, muffled yet echoing. Bos, who had once been a gladiator, turned childish and started a snowball fight, and Curtius, ex Roman centurion, joined in. Afterwards they cleared a path round the cabin, and out to the spring and the latrine hut. Simon was aware of the glow of physical exertion, and the comfortable warmth when they went back inside.

It was three days before the snow stopped. By that time the minimum depth was four feet, and in places it had drifted to more than twice that.

"Right," Brad said. "Ideal conditions."

"Ideal for what?" Simon asked.

"Trying out the showshoes."

They had made the snowshoes out of deerskin and birch saplings, copying those they had seen in the nearby Algonquian village. The manufacture had not been easy, and Simon, who was not particularly skilled at that sort of thing, eventually got bored and abandoned his. Bos took them over and finished them.

Simon had some feeling of guilt about it, which made his response to Brad's proposal less than keen. He pointed out they were due a trading visit from the Indians, and volunteered to stay behind to receive them. The others, after the long confinement, were eager for the open air. He watched them set out up the slope, making clumsy progress.

During the blizzard the chimney vent had provided the only ventilation; the atmosphere was stuffy and, once one had sampled fresh air, unpleasant. Simon drew the bars which secured the wooden shutters and hauled them open. Crisp air flowed in. The light which accompanied it provided all too clear a picture of the squalor arising from their three days of imprisonment, and he decided something must be done about that.

After an hour's cleaning and tidying he was regretting his refusal to go with the others. It wasn't as though they were especially short of food: corn was low, but there was enough for a day or two, and if the Algonquians didn't come to them, they could always go to the village.

But at least the place looked less like a pigsty. He leaned on his broom and stared out at the snow. A jay was busily digging, its white underside blending with the wider white, but the blue top and cocky crested head conspicuous. It dragged something out and flew off with it.

The bird was not only more colourful but sharper looking than the jays he had been used to in England. Thinking that, he realized it was a long time since he had thought much about home: there seemed little point in it, and plenty here to keep his mind occupied. He wondered again what had been made of his and Brad's disappearance; presumably there would have been search parties, rivers and ponds being dragged, all the stuff one saw on television. Television now—that was a strange thing to think of, in this world. He had a sudden sharp awareness of what it might have been like for his folks—Brad's, too—when they failed to come back from that walk. He had always seen his parents as a bit on the cold side—the hugging had come from his granny—but it must have been terrible for them. While as for Granny . . .

There was no point, he told himself once more, in brooding over something one could do nothing about. And it wasn't as though what had happened had been in any way their fault. One moment there had been this weird thing like a fireball, spinning round on the path in front of them; next moment, *wham!* He had blacked out, and when he came round there had been trees around him still, but different trees: a different world.

Gradually he and Brad had pieced things together and come up with an explanation that, however fantastic, fitted the facts of their altered existence. The fireball had been a crossing point between their own world and one which lay on a different probability track—an If world. It was a dizzying thought that there could be an infinite number of such worlds, invisibly side by side.

The one in which they found themselves stemmed from a particular juncture in European history. Here the Roman empire had survived into the late twentieth century, though at a cost of total lack of social or technological progress. The arrival of two people from a highly advanced society had precipitated a revolution, which their special knowledge had helped to succeed. Unfortunately the dictatorship which followed proved much worse than the relatively benevolent tyranny of the empire, threatening them directly.

Brad had been visiting Simon's family in England; his home was in New England, a still undiscovered territory in this world. In view of the situation they were in, it had seemed a good idea to discover America themselves, and they had set sail westwards, taking two Roman friends with them. After a stormy crossing, they had made a landfall in territory inhabited by Algonquian Indians.

Brad, who possessed a near encyclopaedic store of general knowledge which occasionally irritated Simon, knew quite a bit about Indians, especially Algonquians. He even had a smattering of their language, which he had considerably improved during the past months; he could actually converse with them while the other three had to rely almost entirely on sign language. It had been his idea to bring a cargo of trinkets from Europe—beads, metal mirrors, and such—and they had established a useful trade with these for food: the Indians were very effective hunters and also grew corn and a variety of vegetables.

It was really not a bad life, once thoughts of home and technological advantages had been put firmly behind one.

Simon had adapted to it quite well, as had Bos and Curtius, the two Romans. It was Brad who seemed restless and spoke of moving on. He talked of travelling west, across the continent. Simon had considerable doubts as to the advantages of that. He saw no reason to think another place would be better than this, and felt there was a strong possibility of its being worse. Being close to the ocean was vaguely reassuring, too.

Simon's reflections were interrupted by the sight of a deer coming into view at the top of the ridge. It halted there, a beautiful spectacle which also represented food. He made rapid assessment of the possibility of getting within bow shot range before the animal took fright, and decided it was about nil. But there was no harm in trying. He was turning to get his bow when the animal suddenly moved again, but not in flight. It gave a small leap, and dropped. He could see arrow feathers just behind its shoulder: a clean shot.

The Algonquians appeared over the ridge soon after. Two stooped over the deer and the remaining three headed for the hut, the chief, Red Hawk, leading. They too were on snowshoes but there was nothing clumsy or hesitant about their progress. They moved with knees bent, in a shuffling gait that covered the ground almost as fast as a man running.

The usual gestures of greeting were exchanged, and trading started. One of the braves produced the goods they had brought: three rabbits, a haunch of venison, and two birch bark containers of corn out of their winter store. The established tariff was a string of glass beads per container of corn, the same for a rabbit, and two for a haunch of venison. Simon offered seven strings to the chief, and waited for the food to be handed over. The brave who was holding it just stared at him impassively.

Red Hawk spoke a few words and the brave pushed forward a container of corn. That was all right, then. But now Red Hawk handed back four of the strings of beads. Dropping the others into his leather pouch, he pointed to the container Simon had taken and raised his hand with three fingers extended. The significance of the gesture was plain: three strings of beads were required for each container of corn. The exchange rate had taken a bad turn for the worse.

Simon tried pretending this was a misunderstanding. With the container in one hand, he wagged a single finger of the other. The chief stared at him for a long moment, and he thought he might get away with it. Then Red Hawk took the three strings of beads out of his pouch and dropped them on the floor of the hut. He put his hand out for the container.

It was plainly a matter of take it or leave it. He wished the others were there, Brad especially, and looked to see if there was any sign of their returning. But nothing moved apart from the two braves expertly skinning the deer. Red Hawk put his hand on the container, and Simon thought of their depleted grain stock. He raised a hand with two fingers; and Red Hawk stolidly showed three. Simon picked up the three strings of beads and gave them to him.

The others returned a couple of hours later. They untied their snowshoes, and Brad said: "I think I can make it as far as my bed. Just. Funny, my legs are stiff as poles, but the muscles in them have turned to jelly."

Even Bos and Curtius looked exhausted. Simon asked: "Did you find anything?"

"Yes," Curtius said. "A flock of turkeys and a herd of deer. But there were some poor hungry wolves as well, and we thought we would leave it all for them."

Bos pulled off his tunic and wiped sweat from his chest. "It will be better in time. All new things are difficult. We must practise. Today . . ." He shrugged. "We were like tortoises hunting hares."

Brad lay prone on his bed. "How about you? Any sign of Red Hawk?"

Simon nodded. "Yes, he came. They killed a doe up on the ridge."

"I saw blood," Bos said. "They are good hunters."

"What did you buy?" Brad asked.

"A measure of corn."

"Was that all they brought?"

"No. They brought a couple of measures—and rabbits and venison."

Brad sat up. "But we agreed we'd take everything they brought! What's wrong with you?"

"We agreed to buy everything, yes; but not at three times the normal price."

They stared at him.

Curtius asked: "What do you mean?"

He told them.

When he had finished, Brad said: "I wish I'd been here."

"I wish you had, too. But it wouldn't have made any difference. I had a shot at getting him to settle for double instead of triple. He simply reached for the corn."

There was a pause, before Brad said: "Well, we knew corn was going to run short. I guessed we'd have to do without bread towards the end of the winter—the Indians do themselves. I think you should have bought the rest of the stuff, all the same."

"You weren't listening. When I said three times the normal price, that goes for everything."

Brad stared. "You sure?"

"Yes. I checked."

There was a silence. Curtius said: "We must accustom ourselves to those snowshoes quickly then." He sounded gloomy.

Brad said, in an attempt at brightness: "It's not all that bad. So we're on winter tariff now: we still have a margin. There are four sacks of beads left, and the mirrors and the rest. And there's the nanny goat we brought from England, and the hens, to provide milk and eggs. If we're moderately successful hunting and live frugally, we'll be all right."

No one else spoke, and he went on: "We'll do our best to manage without meat from them, but I think we ought to get as much corn in as possible. No, I'm not blaming you, Simon. But we'd better get that other container, even at the new rate." He stretched and yawned. "We're all too bushed to go to the village right now. We'll go first thing tomorrow."

Next morning Simon stayed behind with Bos. He'd decided the sooner he mastered the technique of snowshoeing the better, and Bos volunteered to lend a hand; as was always the case where physical skills were concerned, Bos was the most advanced of them. For two hours they clawed their way up and down the slopes around the hut, until Simon felt like a rag doll that had had its stuffing replaced with lead pellets. He was extremely relieved when the sight of Brad and Curtius returning provided an excuse to break off.

As they got near, though, he could see that the pouch on Brad's back, which should have held the container of corn, was empty. He asked:"What happened?"

"Not enough wampum."

"But you took . . ."

"Three strings: the new rate, as you said." Brad looked grim. "But it seems it's gone up again since yesterday. It's five now."

At the outset Simon, remembering a folklore of flaming arrows, tomahawks, torture, and scalpings and general ferocity, had been very apprehensive of the local Indians. Brad had scornfully dismissed all that as white propaganda, and declared that providing they played fair with the Algonquians, the Algonquians would play fair with them: there was nothing to fear. And as weeks and months had gone by, his argument had been borne out by events. The Indians had shown no sort of aggression and had even invited them, on a couple of occasions, to feasts in the village, in which the longing of Bos and Curtius for the wine they had been used to had to some extent been made up for by a discovery of the joys of tobacco.

The shock when the Indians turned the screw on their food supply was all the greater because of this. They realized they must henceforward live under what amounted to siege conditions. They rationed food strictly and spent every available hour in the search for more. Gradually they accustomed themselves to the snowshoes and got along faster, though they never approached the surefooted speed of the Algonquians.

But game was scarce and grew scarcer. They rarely saw deer, and the section of the forest where turkeys had been abundant didn't offer so much as a feather. Fish, too, seemed to have moved away to warmer waters, and a visit to the lobster pots they had laid off a nearby point revealed a disaster—the lines loose and empty. Assuming the pots had been torn away in the most recent storm, they laboriously set to work making new. When they came back, three days after resetting the pots, they were missing; and the whole of that time the sea had been calm.

Curtius held up a frayed end of rope. It could have frayed against a sharp edge of rock . . . especially with a pair of hands working on it. He said: "You have told us much about these people, Bradus. You have told us they are not thieves but honest dealers. Yet I think someone has taken our pots."

"Wait!"

That was Bos. He scrambled over the rocks and prised something out of a crevice: a broken lobster pot.

Brad stared at it. "No, they aren't thieves. They wouldn't take something that didn't belong to them. But they just might break it up if they decided it was being used to take things *from* them."

"From them?" Curtius was incredulous. "If we steal from anyone, we steal from Neptune!"

Brad said slowly: "They have strange beliefs. I remember something Red Hawk said, at the beginning. He said he had spoken with the gods of land and sea, and we were permitted to enjoy their fruits for the present. The permission to hunt and fish could have been temporary. Maybe he now regards it as withdrawn."

Bos spoke as a Roman Christian: "There is only one God."

Ignoring that, Curtius said: "We Romans have been paying our dues to Neptune for thousands of years. I do not think he will pay any heed to savages."

Brad spoke in English to Simon: "It's not really *gods*, but that was the nearest I could get to it in Latin. They believe in a kind of spiritual essence—*manitou* in Algonquian—a supernatural power that exists not just in people but in things. Things like the sun, moon, thunder, land, and sea. Especially land and sea. In our world, long after the white men had come, some Indians refused to use iron ploughs, in case they bruised mother earth."

The others looked restless, and he went back to Latin: "What matters is that *they* believe in their gods. And if they think the gods don't want us to get lobsters from the sea, they're likely to do what they can to prevent it."

Bos said: "I have seen more Indians than I used to when we have been hunting lately. Maybe they are trying to prevent our getting food from the land, too."

Simon asked: "How?"

"I suppose they could throw a cordon round us," Brad said, "to scare off game before we got within striking distance. Like beaters, only in reverse."

His tone was speculative, but Simon found the thought more chilling than the sub-zero temperature around them. He had already had to get used to the fact that the Algonquians, whom he had envisaged as allies against the North American winter, were taking advantage of it to exploit them. If they were going to be actively hostile, it put a very different complexion on the months ahead.

Curtius said, after a silence: "This is not a good land you have brought us to, Bradus. Things are not as you promised. You spoke of a land of peace and riches, not of cold and hunger and treacherous enemies."

"The land I spoke of is not this one," Brad said. "It lies a long way west of here, on the shore of another ocean. And there, I promise you, we will find all the good things I told you of."

Brad's description of America as an earthly paradise had sustained the two Romans during their voyage towards what they suspected might be the edge of the world. It was probably, Simon thought, not a bad idea to switch the dream to California as an antidote to the grim reality that surrounded them.

"Once we get there, everything will be all right," Brad said. "Believe me."

He was doing it well; he spoke as though he believed it himself. Curtius's look remained sceptical, but Bos said simply: "When do we go there, Bradus?"

"We must wait till the snows have gone."

"If we live so long," Curtius said.

"Things aren't all that bad," Brad said. "At least it's clear they're not going to attack us. They could have done that at any time. We'll just have to outwit them."

"How?" Curtius asked.

"Well, we laid those pots openly. We won't make that mistake again. We'll be more cunning; and in hunting, too."

Simon wondered again how deep his seeming optimism went. For himself he felt cold, and trapped, and more than a bit frightened.

It was soon apparent that outwitting the Algonquians was not going to be easy. They made new lobster pots and set them in a different place at first light, concealing the lines with stones and seaweed. Next day the lines were broken and empty. They took to hunting early and late, as well, and in areas they had not previously visited, but without success. Bos guessed the hut was being kept under surveillance, and the following day, as though in ironic comment, the surveillance became an open one. A brave took up a position on the ridge and stayed there, motionless. When he did go, another took his place, and so it continued from dawn to dusk. Red Hawk had decided they should know they were being watched.

Curtius was more maddened by this than any of them. His instinct, as a trained and experienced Roman soldier, was to attack; he wanted to go up and drive the watcher away, killing him if necessary. The fact that this could only mean a full-scale assault from the rest of the Algonquian braves did not seem to bother him, and Brad and Simon had trouble talking him out of the project. It was a relief that another snowstorm started while they were arguing; even if the Indian remained at his post they could not see him. But they could not go out to hunt, either, with landmarks obliterated by the driving snow.

The storm lasted all day and most of the night. Next morning there was another three feet of snow outside the door. Bos set to work shovelling a path round the hut. Brad was standing by the open door, and Simon joined him.

"No sign of our watcher."

Brad shook his head. "He'll be back."

While they were staring up at the ridge, they heard Bos shout with an urgency that got them running. They rounded the corner of the hut to see him standing in front of the animal pen. He turned towards them, his face showing a mixture of anger and misery.

A section of the pen had been crudely broken, and tracks led away from it across the snow.

Bos said: "I heard sounds in the night, but thought it could have been the wind battering."

"What have we lost?" Brad asked.

"The nanny goat."

"Indians?" Simon asked.

Bos shook his head. "There were paw marks and a trail of blood. A bear."

They stood in silence, taking in this totally unexpected disaster. The nanny, with a kid growing in her belly, had represented a hope for the future. And they had all been fond of her, Bos especially. The big man looked as though he might be going to cry. Possibly in a bid to prevent that, Brad said harshly: "It's a nasty blow. But we couldn't have kept them, once we headed west. The same with the hens. I've known for some time we had to think of them as meat."

Bos surveyed him with heavy eyes. "So we might as well kill the billy now, before the bear comes back, and butcher him for our larder?"

Brad nodded.

"I think I will leave that task to you, Bradus."

Brad did not answer.

Bos fixed his gaze on him for a long moment, then said: "Don't worry. I know what is man's work. I will see to it. You are better skilled at talking. But watch your tongue, boy."

The winter dragged slowly on. The billy goat and chickens provided a temporary addition to their food supplies; while they lasted, they did not need to buy meat from the Indians and could conserve the diminishing supply of wampum. There was still a watcher on the ridge, though, and the snares they set stayed empty. Red Hawk had suspended his visits, but uncannily, as though he knew the exact contents of their larder, he returned when they were down to the last chicken and the last haunch of goat meat. His rates had gone up again, and a lot more winter lay ahead. There was a brief period of milder weather, but it was followed by a series of bitter storms which kept them inside the cabin, in unhappy and hungry confinement.

The next clear spell saw Red Hawk back with his braves. They brought two rabbits and some withered roots. He wanted twelve strings of beads for each of the rabbits. For the roots—he gestured magnanimously—three only.

They were stunned into silence. Red Hawk's face was expressionless as usual; then, astonishingly, it cracked into a smile. He pointed at Bos, and spoke to Brad. Simon picked up the occasional word: *hair . . . knife . . . wampum . . .* Brad was asking, offering, finally appealing. The smile went from Red Hawk's face, and there was no mirth in Brad's. At the end, he said to the others: "Get them the wampum. Twenty-seven strings."

"We are on the last sack," Bos said.

"I know." Brad shrugged. "We have no choice."

The weather had cleared to a frozen calm, and they had the shutters open. They watched the Indians travel easily up the slope and over the ridge. Turning away, Brad said: "Well, that's that."

Simon said: "Tell us the worst."

"I was going to." He paused. "The first bit was joke time, Algonquian style. He said we needn't pay wampum for the roots. They would take Bos's beard in exchange."

To the Indians, who plucked out what little facial hair they had, Bos's curly and luxuriant beard had been a source of interest from the beginning; they had grown used to the women and children giggling over it when they visited the village. Bos uttered a Roman curse. Brad said: "I refused the offer politely, and Red Hawk said they would not hurt him by hacking it off with their poor stone knives; they would buy our strange sharp ones and use them. For two knives they would bring us a turkey. I said no, we would not sell the knives, and he said it didn't matter anyway."

Brad took a deep breath. "That was when I offered him the cabin."

They stared at him. Simon said: "You did what?"

"I explained that we would be moving on, as soon as the snows melted. I said that if they would give us food until the spring we would give them the cabin then, and some knives, and an axe, and other valuable things. Things which were our possessions, which belonged to us."

Simon said: "I suppose . . ."

Brad went on: "He said it was true these objects were ours, but only as long as the Great Spirit continued to breathe life into our mouths. Dead men, he said, had no possessions. Before the winter ended, we would be dead. Then any man might take things which no longer had an owner."

After a pause, Bos said: "As you told us, they are not thieves. They only starve men to death, then take their goods."

Curtius said: "I have had enough of this. Let us attack them, while the strength is in us. I would rather die as a soldier than as a famished rat!"

Bos growled approval.

Brad said: "I agree about doing something while we still have the strength. But something better than committing suicide, which is what that would amount to. One possibility would be to abandon the cabin now and head south."

Simon said: "That gets my vote. This place has become a death trap. And providing we don't freeze to death, heading south means heading for the sun. It's the best chance we have."

"Except for one thing," Brad said.

"What?"

"Red Hawk thought we might think of that. He said if we left, he would send braves to follow us. They would keep us in sight as long as we were in Algonquian lands, and when we left those lands, they would return to report our deaths. Because the next lands to the south are inhabited by the Iroquois, who kill strangers. They do this slowly, but he can be certain that within a week we will be dead. Knowing that, they will feel entitled to take possession of the cabin, and everything in it."

Bos said: "I will take that chance, sooner than starve here."

"I, too," said Curtius. "And I think we will kill a few of the Iroquois before they kill us."

"I might agree," Brad said, "if there were no alternative."

Simon said: "Starving to death, freezing to death, getting killed in an attack on the Algonquians, being tortured to death by Iroquois . . . not just alternatives: we have a multiple choice."

Brad ignored him. "North and west, Algonquians, for hundreds of miles. South, more Algonquians, followed by Iroquois who seem to be rather worse. There's still east."

"Sure," Simon said, "the ocean. Three thousand miles of it. Quite a swim."

An early storm had brought seas sweeping high up the beach to batter a hole in the side of the ship which had brought them from England, and later storms had completed her destruction. Curtius in particular had been depressed by the loss of this solitary link with his homeland, remaining gloomy for days.

Brad said: "You know how cold the water's been here, even in summer? It's caused by a strong current from the north that skirts this coast. The *Stella*'s finished, but we could make a raft out of her timbers. The current will take it south. We might be able to miss Iroquois territory altogether. At least we'll be heading towards a better climate."

He looked around at their faces.

"What do you think?"

"I think," Bos said, "that we will start right away."

It wasn't easy; it was murderously difficult, in fact. They had to break the *Stella* up to get at the deck timbers. Although it didn't snow, the wind remained easterly, howling over the grey breakers and peppering them with freezing darts of spray.

When the raft was half-built, the disheartening realization came that it was not only well above the tide mark but would be too heavy to drag down once completed: they were obliged to break it up and begin again at the water's edge, with bitterly cold waves breaking over their legs. They took turns in going back to the hut to thaw themselves out. Then they had to drive in heavy stakes to anchor it against being carried away by the incoming tide.

All this time they were under observation by the Algonquians. Since the purpose of their activity was so obvious, Simon wondered whether the Indians might intervene to stop them, but they never approached nearer than a couple of hundred yards. The reason, it eventually occurred to him, was that, in Red Hawk's view, putting out to sea on a raft was the equivalent of going into Iroquois territory, as far as the outcome was concerned: the moment they did it, they were as good as dead. He straightened up from hammering and looked across the heaving swell. It seemed to stretch into eternity, grey sea merging into grey sky. Red Hawk was probably right, at that.

At last it was finished. They stacked what was worth taking with them, including the meagre store of food, in the centre of the raft. Curtius wanted to set fire to the cabin, but the others said no: it might provoke the Indians to see their prospective spoils going up in smoke. The last thing Bos took was a pouch, which he tied securely to his belt. In it were roots of vines in a protective cocoon of moss. He had brought them with him from the Emperor's own vineyard in Rome, and his promise to himself was that someday, in some place, they would grow, and flower, and fruit; and he would make wine from the grapes.

It only remained to float the raft. That wasn't easy, either. They had to struggle, knee-deep in near freezing water, to move it. At last it bobbed clear, and they scrambled on board. It was about fifteen feet across, with a low surrounding gunnel. It would have been a mad idea for four men to entrust their lives to such a craft even on a placid lake in summer. They had erected a small mast and had a sail but could not use it with the wind blowing steadily towards shore. They paddled the raft out through the breakers.

It helped a bit when they could strip off their soaked clothes and put on dry. The ridge beyond the reach was crowded now with figures; Simon thought he recognized Red Hawk in the centre of them. Gradually they dwindled in size and began to fall away astern.

"That's it!" Brad said. "We're in the current—heading south."

2

THE MOTION WAS UNPLEASANT to begin with, and rapidly got worse. Simon would have been sick if there had been anything in his stomach; as it was, he spent a long time retching helplessly over the side of the raft. All their faces, in the fading light, had a greenish grey look. They bobbed along about half a mile off a shore so featureless that it was hard to believe they were making any progress. Past the sea's heaving grey, the land was a white desert.

When darkness fell, they huddled together to keep warm; but seas slopped over the gunnel and from time to time a wave drenched them. Nausea gradually gave way to ravening hunger. They chewed dried meat and sipped water from a leather flask, though sparingly. It was bitter and resinous, but very precious. They could die of thirst, if cold and exhaustion did not do the job first.

The night was wretched. They had been mad, Simon decided, to fall in with Brad's scheme. Even if they had starved to death in the hut, they would at least have been dry and warm, with solid ground beneath them. He felt a resentment which, as the hours ground by, turned to something close to hate. It was not just the raft. Brad had been the one who assured them that the Indians were trustworthy, just as it had been Brad who had come up with the crazy idea of a voyage to discover America. In fact, going back to the beginning; it had been Brad who had insisted on going forward to investigate the fireball, instead of doing the sensible thing and backing away from it.

Bos had managed to fall asleep and was snoring. Curtius was groaning softly.

Brad said suddenly: "I think the sky's lightening."

Angrily Simon said: "Shut up. We've had enough out of you."

"Over there."

He could barely make out Brad's pointing arm. It was ridiculous; the night was as stygian as ever. But as he peered it did seem that the blackness might be slightly less in that quarter. Or was it an illusion?

Bos, who had woken up, said: "It is the beginning of dawn." He sighed vastly. "It will be good to see land."

"And when we do," Simon said, "we make for it, whatever kind of Indians are waiting."

Curtius groaned again. "I agree. Any place, even Hades, sooner than this."

As light slowly grew in the east, Simon strained his eyes in the opposite direction, where the coast must lie. The others were doing the same. Bos stood up, his arm around the mast. It was he who said at last, in a tight grim voice: "There is no land."

Simon stood up too, holding on to the big Roman as the raft rolled. He gazed to the west; far across the waves sea and sky came together, with nothing breaking their union. Although he knew it was pointless, he stared south and north as well. There was nothing but churning water and an empty sky.

Curtius said bitterly: "That was something else you promised us, Bradus—a current that runs close by the shore and will carry us south to warmer lands. Where is it?"

"I don't know."

Brad's voice was dull; his old ebullience had gone completely. Great stuff, Brad, Simon thought, from the guy who knows all the answers. But he felt too wretched to voice it.

Bos pointed something else out: the wind had changed and was coming from the southwest. They could not use the sail to any purpose. Bos proposed using the paddles, but did not persist in the notion when he failed to get any support. They were all close to exhaustion, and the effort seemed pointless against the surrounding vastness of the ocean.

All day they drifted, seeing nothing except the occasional sea bird. Simon was slightly encouraged by the sight of the first until he recalled that many birds, such as petrels and shearwaters, thought nothing of crossing the Atlantic. This one was too far away to be identifiable.

Night fell a second time, and they huddled together in silence. Eventually fatigue overcame discomfort, and Simon drifted off. He dozed fitfully, then suddenly awoke, confused and disoriented but aware of light. The sky had cleared; there was a new moon low down, and the constellations gleamed overhead. He managed to pick out the Plough, and from that the North Star. It was on his right, and he thought that must mean they were heading west, towards land. Then he remembered this was a raft not a boat, with neither bow nor stern, and no fixed external point to serve as a reference: there was no way of knowing in which direction they were travelling.

He slipped back into sleep. His next awakening was more abrupt. He had a sensation of something being close by; and looked and saw it. A hillock stood up, black against the moonlight, seeming almost close enough to reach out and touch. Land! He cried out, and Bos answered: "What is it, lad?"

"The paddles! It's . . ."

He broke off. He could see another hillock dead ahead and a third way over to the right. He could also see that the hillocks were relatively small, and surrounded by water. Suddenly the one nearest slowly sank beneath the waves.

"Whales." Bos's voice was tensely calm. "We are inside a pack of them."

They no longer looked small. Not far from where that one had submerged, another rose enormously. Simon reminded himself he had always been in favour of whales—that they were intelligent and peaceable creatures. But his instinctive reaction to these vast things coming out of the sea was terror.

Whispering, Brad said: "Better keep quiet. They have good hearing."

Hoping for reassurance, Simon asked: "But they're harmless, aren't they?"

"Depends what you call harmless. If they just got curious, it might not be funny."

Simon saw the point. None of them spoke as the whales slid by, roller coasting in and out of the waves. And as time went by and nothing happened he began to feel less frightened. However large the pack, they must come to an end of it eventually. Was that open water, beyond the next dark hulk?

Then he cried out as the timbers beneath him tilted without warning. The raft lifted and twisted and he felt himself falling backwards. He grasped for the mast and managed to get a hold, but lost it when Bos involuntarily cannoned into him and knocked him away. Sliding again, he hit the gunnel and made an unsuccessful grab at that. He sank into stingingly cold water and felt his nostrils fill as he went deep down.

He had no coherent thoughts, but his arms moved of their own volition, beating a way back to the surface. He broke water and gasped in breath. With a shock of despair, he saw empty sea before him: no whales, but no raft either.

The call came from behind, and he turned, treading water. The raft was about thirty yards away but it seemed a lot further; beyond it, one of the retreating whales blew a spume of spray into the moonlight. The cold bit deeper as he swam towards the raft, and his arms felt more leaden with each stroke. He had an impulse to ease up, let go—wasn't drowning supposed to be an easy death? But he heard their voices urging him on, Bos bellowing above the rest, and managed to keep going. His senses were hazing when his fingers touched wood and he felt them hauling him on board; his teeth chattered and he was shivering violently. Bos and Brad joined arms around him, holding his cold wet body between theirs.

They held him in that fashion till daybreak. This time there was a sunrise, but he could take no interest in the golden disk slowly lifting from the horizon. He felt it had no heat in it; despite the warmth of other bodies, chillness held him in a vice. He heard the others talking, but their words were meaningless. Bos tried to make him eat, but it was too much effort. The climbing sun was turning the sea's grey to green, but he felt indifferent to it, to everything except the paralyzing cold.

Even when Bos shouted "Land!" it meant nothing. They left him to scramble for the paddles and he had the vague thought that he ought to lend a hand, but all his energy was taken up in shivering. He drifted along the edge of consciousness. After a long time he was aware that Brad and Bos were holding him again, and that the raft still floated. So there was no landfall after all. It didn't matter: nothing mattered.

He fell eventually into a deep sleep. Awaking he felt a bit better and even managed to sit up. The sun was at its zenith; and while he was far from warm, the cold was not quite so bitter. He felt thirsty and asked for water. He learned something unpleasant then. The amphora which was the main freshwater container had gone overboard when he did. Only the contents of the flask were left—a few mouthfuls each.

He asked about the land Bos had sighted. They told him it had been in view upwards of an hour, but though they had fancied at first they were making progress towards it, the current had carried them on past. He said: "I ought to have helped."

Bos shrugged. "It would have made no difference. A kitten would have pulled as strongly. Eat, Simonus, so you can help next time."

While he chewed on a piece of meat, Brad spoke to him in English: "I was right about the current. What I got wrong was our original position. I figured we were somewhere on the Maine coast, but I realize now we must have been much further north—Nova Scotia, probably. The current did take us south-west, but across open sea. The land we saw was probably Cape Cod. And if we're on the same drift, there's a chance of making Nantucket. We've three or four hours of daylight, and that should be enough to give us a sighting."

Simon started to reply, but was prevented by a cry from Curtius.

"Look over there! Is that land?"

There was something, certainly, that was neither sea nor sky. Sunlight glinted from a long level whiteness. They were drifting slowly towards it.

It was Bos who spoke: "No, not land. Sea mist."

As they got nearer, its appearance became less uniform; there were rifts and eddyings. Tendrils of mist began to curl up out of the sea. The sun dimmed, brightened slightly, dimmed further. It was a disk of pale yellow, of white and barely visible against the white all round; then it was gone. The mist hemmed them in completely, a filthy grey now and sharply chilling.

They could see no more than a few yards from the raft's edge. Even if Brad's guess had been right, they could pass within fifty yards—fifty feet—of land and never know it. The mist had robbed them of the few remaining hours of daylight. After that there would be night again, and open sea.

No one felt like talking; even Bos, who had previously been a source of encouragement, fell silent. The only sound was the slap of water against the raft's timbers. Somewhere overhead the sun was moving relentlessly down to its setting. Time passed. How long had it been, Simon wondered—one hour, two? Three, even? Was the mist beginning to darken? He had a feeling it was.

The apparition that unexpectedly loomed over them was frightening in quite a different way from the whales. The size of the creatures against the smallness of the raft had been the main factor then. This was something of a different order: a shock of realizing that fairy stories, nightmares, could come true. The incredible head of the sea serpent gaped down at them, with gleaming teeth. Simon's own cry of fear was lost in those of the rest. And there were other sounds—shouts coming out of the mist. Wood splintered, and he had time to see a broken oar flail through the air towards his head before the raft jerked and lifted, and once again he found himself tossed into the sea.

Simon was first to be picked up, but the rest quickly followed. Brad and Curtius had managed to cling to the raft's mast, while Bos had grabbed the broken oar of the dragon ship as a spar. Once they had been hauled on board they could get a good look at their rescuers. They were big and blond and hairy, with drooping moustaches and curly beards. But physical appearance apart, the horned helmets identified them, as, of course, the ship itself had done once Simon realized it wasn't a sea monster. They were Vikings.

That left a lot of questions unanswered. To begin with, what was a longship doing three thousand miles from the area in which one would expect to find it? And how did it happen that the language being spoken by the Vikings was not some Scandinavian tongue, but a corrupt form of the Latin spoken in Europe on this side of the fireball?

The most important thing, though, was that despite their barbarous looks, and the stone axes hung in a long row inside the gunnels, they seemed amiable. A horn was offered round, and proved to contain a sweet, warming ale. Another Viking produced from a chest tunics of soft skin to replace their wet clothing. And although their version of Latin was not too easy to follow, there was no doubt they were expressing pleasure at having been able to snatch the four of them from the sea's clutches.

Simon said to Brad: "I don't get it. Do you have any idea where they come from?"

"Wherever it is, not too far away. I heard one of them say that but for the mist they wouldn't have found us—they'd have been back in home harbour two hours ago."

"Home harbour? On this side of the Atlantic?"

"I've been trying to figure that out. Of course, there was speculation in our world that the Vikings could have crossed the Atlantic. There was the theory that some of them reached what they called Vinland, which was probably not far from where we landed. And what may have been Viking artifacts were discovered in the Great Lakes area. So there's no reason why they shouldn't have crossed the ocean on this side of the fireball, too. On the other hand . . ." He was looking puzzled.

Simon said: "On the other hand, what?"

"Our Viking Age began about 800 A.D.—that's more than four hundred years after the Emperor Julian. And it's generally accepted that what permitted them to swarm across Europe was the weakness, in fact the disintegration of the Frankish empire. But the Frankish empire only came into being after the Roman empire collapsed . . . and in *this* world it didn't collapse. So where do these Vikings come from?"

"I don't see the problem. Even in this world, the Romans didn't occupy the whole of Europe. Bos was born free as a barbarian in north Britain. In fact, most of Scandinavia isn't under Roman rule, so why couldn't they simply have crossed from there?"

"Ye-es. There's just one little thing that bothers me about that."

"Go on."

"If their original home was outside the empire, why are they speaking Latin, rather than Norse?"

Simon thought about it. "So what is the answer?"

"I don't know. I suppose we'll find out eventually. The good news is that we *can* talk to them. And that these natives definitely are friendly."

While the longship wallowed idly, the Vikings chatted and passed round the horn of ale, replenishing it from time to time from a wooden barrel. They didn't seem concerned about being immobilized by the mist; the sea was flat calm and longships were provisioned for long periods at sea. Food was provided: dried meat, salt fish, and a kind of biscuit. Once he had warmed up, Simon realized how hungry he was and ate ravenously.

He found the guttural, distorted Latin more comprehensible as he got used to it. Their rescuers clearly knew of the lands on the far side of the ocean and assumed they were castaways from a ship which had gone astray. But they showed no real curiosity about them. They were more interested when Bos spoke of the pack of whales. It seemed that whale hunting had been the object of their expedition, but they had found none.

Gradually the mist thinned and the sun's faint disk appeared close to the horizon. Talk was abandoned for the oars, and the longship headed southwest to the pull of hairy arms. They sang as they rowed, in a rhythmic chant matching the beat of the blades. Only two were absent from the benches: a wiry scar-faced man at the tiller and a big man with a gold chain round his neck, who was plainly the captain. He stood on a wooden platform just behind the dragon's neck, fixing his gaze on the waters ahead.

The sun was below the horizon and the day fast darkening when he aroused cheers with the cry of "Land in sight!" The mist had completely cleared, and despite the dusk a low line of coast was plainly visible on the port bow. Their progress was fast, and it was not long before they were rounding a headland, the point of a long peninsula. Course was altered southerly; they approached another spur of land, enclosing a broad harbour.

Brad said: "I was right."

"About what?" Simon asked.

"The harbour's unmistakable. Yankees went whaling from here, too. That's Nantucket island."

"Home," the Viking captain said, smiling broadly. "Warm hearths, warm hearts, good food, and good cheer! Welcome, friends."

The town, or more correctly village, stood directly over the harbour, looking down to the quay where the longships were moored to tall posts topped with ornamental heads that matched the ships' figureheads. There were two or three hundred wooden huts, set higgledy-piggledy around a larger longer building. There was no road as such, but paths twisted in and out of the huts. Many generations of feet had worn them down below the original level, and each hut stood on a small knoll of earth. Whatever the reason for the Vikings' coming here, it had happened a long time ago. Simon looked at the huts as they trooped past them. They had been solidly built in the first place, but many seemed in need of repair. A gaping crack in one had been plugged with hides.

Women and children thronged out to welcome their menfolk back. They, too, were blonde, the women large-boned with braids of yellow hair that framed plump pink cheeks. They favoured the strangers with curious looks. And a buxom lady who, judging from the way she embraced him, was the captain's wife, asked where they came from.

He roared laughter. "From the sea—a gift from Odin. But in truth, wife, they come from beyond the great water, as our forefathers did. They are Romans! Romans will grace the winter feast this year. Is that not good news?"

She answered his laugh with one equally hearty. The other women crowded close, staring at the Romans, even fingering them. One patted Brad's cheek and another twined fingers in Bos's beard. Simon came in for some prodding which he did not care for; he reflected, though, that it was better than the attentions they would have been likely to receive at the hands of the Iroquois squaws. Then he saw something which took his mind off the Iroquois.

She stood back from the rest. She was about fourteen but as tall as he was. Her hair was a brighter, more buttery gold than that of the others, her eyes a purer cornflower blue. And there was a charming earnestness about her gaze. Simon returned the look and thought she coloured slightly.

Then she turned and went, disappearing behind one of the huts.

Following her with his eyes, Simon noticed something: Brad was doing the same.

They feasted that night in the large building, which was both a general meeting place and the assembly point for their tribal council, the *thing*. A stone hearth at the centre supported a big log fire; the men sat at tables on either side and the women brought round food and drink.

The drink, which they were told was made from honey, tasted like a dryish wine. A variety of food was ladled onto the wooden platters: different kinds of preserved fish, spicy sausages, baked fish, and chunks of roast meat which proved to be whale. Pickled vegetables and corn bread were served with them.

With his belly pleasantly full, Simon paid more attention to his surroundings. The hall was very old: the table had been worn into hollows by generations of elbows. High on the walls were hung overlapping rows of round shields —hundreds of them, perhaps thousands. The lighting was from smoky lamps which gave off a pungent smell; whale oil, he supposed. In their glow he could see dozens of whalebone and seal tusks, intricately carved.

He was looking for the girl but did not see her. Most of the women were quite old; he guessed they were wives of the warriors and that unmarried girls were not allowed at the feasts. It was a pity, but there would be time to see her again. Perhaps quite a lot of time. The thought of staying here permanently crossed his mind, followed by the thought that he could think of many worse things. Staying, of course, would depend on being invited, but the remarks of the captain—who had proved to be the Viking chief, Wulfgar—about a gift from Odin sounded promising.

They had been given seats of honour close by the chief, and Bos now addressed him, thanking him and complimenting him on the quality of his hospitality. He said: "It is not just for food and drink that we owe you thanks, though it is a long time since I dined so well." He patted his belly, belching appreciatively. "Death would have found us, had you not found us first."

"The finding was our good fortune," Wulfgar said. He wagged a greasy fist clutching a chunk of meat. "I have been favoured by the gods before, but never so greatly."

That seemed excessive, Simon thought, but it was probably just a fashion of talking. He decided to follow the custom of the country and weigh in with a little hyperbole himself. He felt quite proud of his eloquence, as he emptied his pot and had it immediately refilled by one of the Viking women. He waved it in the air, spilling a few drops on Brad beside him.

"For all these things," he concluded grandly, "we are most deeply in your debt, and not least for being honoured as guests at your winter feast."

He had a feeling that a lot of what he had said had been less than perfectly intelligible—their versions of Latin were still considerably at cross purposes—but Wulfgar at least picked up his last words.

"Our winter feast?" The chief's face broadened in another laugh. "But this is not our winter feast, Roman! It wants another month till Yule. Then we have *real* eating and drinking, in celebration of the turn of the year."

Bos turned his eyes up. "I could not fill my belly fuller than I have tonight."

"The turn of the year," Wulfgar repeated, "and thanks to your coming, the turn in our fortunes."

His wife was at his elbow, and refilled his pot, too. Wulfgar drank deeply, then upended it, emptying the lees into the rushes that covered the floor of the hall. The gesture was harsh and brutal, for a moment almost menacing. But he laughed again, and his warriors laughed with him.

"To Odin," he cried, "the bringer of gifts!"

3

BRAD HAD VISITED the island before, on the other side of the fireball; when he and Simon set off next morning on a trip of exploration, he marvelled at the emptiness of the beaches.

"That one was jammed with tourists—hot dog vendors, ice cream vans, the works. And the bay dotted with small boats. Big ones, too—forty and fifty footers."

Earlier both sea and island had been mist-covered, but the rising sun had burnt it away. There was haze at the horizon, but close at hand everything was clear and sharp and brightly glinting.

Simon felt cheerful. He said: "Red Hawk's turning nasty seems to have been all for the best, doesn't it? We'd have had the winter to get through and after that a transcontinental trek, with no guarantees of the kind of reception we might get on the way."

Brad looked at him sharply. "You thinking of staying on here?"

"It's crossed my mind." Brad said nothing. "The climate in California may be better, but we've no idea what other conditions are like. At least here we're among civilized people—well, fairly civilized. And we can speak the language. It may have been OK for you, but I was never going to get by in Algonquian."

They were walking along a ridge with views both inland and over the bay. The landscape was bare, mostly scrub. Brad said: "We don't know we can stay."

"I reckon we'll be welcome, as long as we do our bit."

"Lend a hand with the whaling?"

"That, and whatever else is needed."

Brad kicked a stone and watched it roll down the slope towards the beach.

"I've been trying to work out their economy," he said. "There's all this wood they use—for houses, boats, and so on—and yet the island's badly off for trees—always has been. And the wood they've used is mostly pine, which I doubt would thrive here. Then there was the food last night. The fish figures, and I guess they can grow vegetables; but I'd be surprised if they could grow enough corn to see them through the winter, and there was no shortage of bread. I saw beehives in a field on the other side of the village—that explains the honey for the mead, and as a sweetener generally. But what about clothing? They dress in skins—but where do they get the skins? Seal, sure, and there's probably local jackrabbit, but I saw others. There was beaver, and I'll swear this isn't beaver country. And those big rugs in the hall were bearskin."

"They probably trade with Indians on the mainland."

"They must. Bartering whale products, most likely. Whale's a very useful commodity: you get meat, blubber, whale skin and whale bone. Whale oil, too. That would account for the timber and stuff. I guess you could buy a forest with a single whale. But how would you transport it? Longships don't have much of a cargo capacity."

"Does it matter?"

There were times when Brad's passion for facts and origins was more than a little tedious.

"I'd like to know."

"Well, if we stay here you'll no doubt find out."

They crossed the narrow part of the island and threw stones at the sea from one of the southern beaches before heading back towards the village. At the point where they entered it, one of the huts was being rebuilt, with timber cannibalized from a derelict hut nearby. The workers were all female. Simon said: "Do you think we should offer to lend a hand? Might make a good impression."

"The question," Brad said, "is whether it would *be* a good impression. There may be a tradition about the division of labour—men hunting the whales, women doing the construction work . . . that type of thing. Butting in might not be a good idea."

The women, certainly, looked eminently capable; many were brawnier than the Viking men. One or two glanced in their direction, but most were engrossed in their tasks.

Brad said: "Better not hang around."

They started to move on, then stopped. The girl they had seen the previous day appeared from behind the hut which was being dismantled. She had a wooden billet across her shoulders. It was over six feet long and a couple of feet wide: the weight of it bowed her.

Possibly as a result of catching sight of them, she suffered a temporary loss of balance. She staggered and eased the billet off her shoulders onto the ground. While Simon was still thinking about it, Brad sprinted across and took hold of the billet. She stepped back, smiling, and he stooped to pick it up.

At least he tried. Contorting himself, he managed to get it off the ground and staggered about in a comic dance for two or three seconds before being forced to set it down. Simon saw the girl start to smile again. So did Brad, and with a tremendous effort he got it onto his shoulder. He even managed a few steps carrying it, but it was unevenly balanced and he had to let it go before it pulled him over.

Simon took the wood from him; Brad was too busy getting his breath back to protest.

Simon bent his knees and heaved. He succeeded in lifting it onto his right shoulder. It rested about as lightly as a stone obelisk, and not one of the smaller kind. With carefully measured tread, trying not to wince from the pain, he crossed to the hut and set it down with great relief. Brad and the girl had followed him. The smile she gave him made him feel better, but he was glad the hut had not been ten yards further away. Or two, for that matter.

It seemed a good opportunity for introductions; he told her his name and Brad's, and she gave hers. She was Lundiga, daughter of Sigrid. Simon would have been glad to prolong the chat, but an older woman called her to help with heaving a beam into place. When Simon tried to assist, Lundiga shook her head firmly. "It is not proper."

As they walked on, Simon said: "Isn't she terrific?"

"Great," Brad said, "if you're into weightlifters."

"The weightlifters I've seen weren't as pretty."

Brad said sourly: "Maybe not. Kissing her would still be something like being hugged by a grizzly."

"I wouldn't mind taking the chance. You don't meet a lot of bears with a face like that—or figure."

"I'd watch it if I were you."

"That wouldn't be sour grapes?"

"No," Brad said. "Good advice. Lundiga, daughter of Sigrid . . ."

"Well?"

"If you'd been paying attention yesterday, you'd know Sigrid is Wulfgar's wife. Which makes Lundiga the daughter of the chief."

"Ah." Simon thought about it. "On the other hand, where's the harm in making friends with the boss's daughter?"

Bos and Curtius quickly adjusted to life on the island. This was not really surprising, since it was basically a life of ease. While the women worked, the Viking men sat around and gossiped; down by the boats when the weather was fine, otherwise in the hall. There was much talk and laughter, singing and long-winded declamations of verse, and a vast amount of drinking either mead or strong ale. They also played a variation of the Roman dice and counter game.

Talking in the hut which had been allocated them, Curtius said: "For the first time, Bradus, I do not regret that we crossed the ocean. A man can be at peace in such a land as this."

Brad said: "We've not been here long. Life can't be all wine and dice."

That was the Latin equivalent of beer and skittles.

Curtius said: "I do not look for life to be all wine and dice. I will be happy to hunt the great sea beasts alongside men like these Vikings. This is a good place, with good people. Your own land in the west may have all the wonders you have spoken of, but you have also said it lies a long journey away. It is reasonable that you two should wish to return to your homeland, but things are different for us. Eh, Bos?"

Bos yawned mightily. Simon had left the pair of them carousing in the hall the night before, and been awakened by their drunken return in the small hours.

Bos said: "Yes, this life will do for me."

Brad said: "It's a poor soil and a cold climate for those vines of yours."

He nodded towards the shelf where the pouch with the vine roots lay.

Bos said: "You may be right. And it's true I would prefer a flask of good Falernian to the brew they serve here. But it is not so long since the best liquor on offer was melted snow. When a man offers you a beast, you do not look too closely at its teeth, especially if there is no other within a year's trudging."

Simon's private objective was seeing more of Lundiga, and this did not prove too difficult. What was difficult, though, in fact seemingly impossible, was to see her on her own. There was no problem when other women were present, or even when there were just the two of them plus Brad, but attempts to put their acquaintance on any more intimate basis were smilingly but resolutely resisted. "It is not proper, Simonus."

He reflected gloomily that she took propriety a good deal too seriously, but it was a pleasure to look at her even when she was reproving him. She was certainly not a small girl, but very well proportioned; and the golden hair, blue eyes, and strawberries-and-cream complexion completed a picture that delighted the eye. She matched Simon inch for inch in height, which meant Brad had to look up to her. There was nothing wrong with that, either.

The Viking women were hard workers. Apart from tidying and cleaning, preparing food, looking after children and animals, and tending things in general, they kept the huts in repair, brought in fuel for the fires, and cleared paths between the huts when it snowed. They even laid fishing lines in the harbour and mended the sails of the longships.

The men, on the other hand, did absolutely nothing. Simon, embarrassed by the contrast of hard work and bone idleness, asked Lundiga if there was not some way in which he could help. She shook her head decisively. "It is not proper."

And yet Simon did not feel the women were dominated; he had an impression, from looks and occasional critical remarks, that their attitude towards their menfolk was more one of mild contempt than submission. A reply by Lundiga to a query from Brad about the number of unoccupied huts in the village tended to confirm this.

In olden days, she said, the men had been true warriors, and explorers and traders, taking their longships on frequent voyages to the mainland. Whaling, too, had been more keenly pursued, and more successful. Nowadays they were increasingly loath to put to sea, and returned empty-handed as often as not. Brad asked how they had brought timber from the mainland. They had tied tree trunks together in rafts, she explained, and towed them. But that had been abandoned; for more than a generation no new timber had been brought in, which was why the women had to repair the huts with bits from unused ones. In fact, many huts were empty. Fewer children were being born, so the number of the people dwindled.

When they were alone, Brad said to Simon: "They're dying out, that's for sure."

"Why, do you think?"

"Could be one of several things, or a combination. In our world a Norse colony flourished on Greenland for four centuries, then suddenly went. No one was certain why. Climatic changes maybe. That could be happening here. Or the effects of interbreeding. Or just plain lethargy. They've been doing the same things at the same season for a thousand years or more, on a tiny island. They may just be bored with it all."

Simon said: "Things may have gone on without changing for a thousand years, but there's a change now."

Brad looked at him. "What would that be?"

"Our being here."

"You think that will make a difference?"

"It might."

Brad said thoughtfully: "You'd think with the women doing all the work they'd be totally subservient, but it's not like that. The men are served by the women, and boast about their whale hunts, and make the big noises generally. But children are identified through their mother, not their father. Lundiga, daughter of Sigrid—even though Wulfgar's the chief. And did you hear what she was saying this morning: that where marriage is concerned the women do the choosing?"

"Yes, I heard."

There had been no particular significance in Lundiga's expression when she was imparting this information, but it had happened not long after Simon had been telling her that in all his worldwide travels he had never met a girl as beautiful as she was.

"And, as I say," Brad said, "she's the chief's daughter. So who comes next as chief—Simonus, the saviour of the Vikings?"

Brad dodged the blow aimed at him, and Simon let it go at that. He didn't really object to the remark.

Whaling was a constant preoccupation with the Vikings, but a preoccupation displayed more in talk than action. There were rambling yarns, drinking around the fire at night, of past expeditions—of chasings and killings and which hero had cast the harpoon which laid the great beast low. From that, drinking more deeply, they would go on to the next trip, which they would make tomorrow or, if something happened to prevent it, the day after. Something always did happen. The sea was too smooth, which meant the whales would hide in the mists, or there was a swell which meant they would be swimming deep, or a blizzard was threatening. Or the Vikings just did not wake up early enough.

At last, though, on a bright morning with a stiff wintry breeze from the south, they actually got going. Lundiga had told Simon and Brad her mother was worried about stocks, in particular oil, and they thought she might have had a private word with Wulfgar. At any rate all three seaworthy longships were manned by the full complement of men, apart from four manifestly too old and feeble and a fifth who had broken a leg in the course of drunken acrobatics. Lundiga said she could remember when four ships had gone out, and in her grandfather's day there had been six: several dilapidated hulks were rotting at the quayside.

The newcomers had been split up, but Simon and Brad found themselves together on Wulfgar's ship. The oar Simon manned was longer and heavier than he had been used to in school rowing, and he found it hard going. Once clear of the harbour, though, the sail was raised and they could relax. The sail had a depiction of a dragon, too, in faded scarlet paint. They headed northwest, pounding along under a sky that offered rapid alternations of blue and quite thick cloud. The sea was choppy, but the ship's motion was not too bothersome, and after a time Simon found it exhilarating.

Scarface, as before, took the tiller, while Wulfgar shouted commands from his look-out platform. His voice was powerful and needed to be for him to make himself heard above the oarsmen's din. When they weren't singing, they were engrossed in chatter and the exchange of ribald insults. Your average Viking might lay claim to being a strong man, Simon thought, but you could scarcely call him silent.

After some hours of uneventful sailing, they ate: bread and meat were passed along the benches, with flasks of water and ale. Simon confined himself to water, but the Vikings were downing great draughts of ale. The flask was emptied and refilled, a process that was repeated more than once. The oarsmen grew even noisier and more garrulous and, in some cases, combative. Two on the opposite side, near Brad's oar, started a fight which Wulfgar was obliged to come aft to deal with. He grabbed a neck in either hand and slammed their horned helmets together with a resounding crack, bellowing oaths. They meekly subsided.

It was not long after that he raised the cry of "*Balleinus!*" indicating a whale in view. The Vikings roared drunken approval, and Wulfgar chanted a time for the oars, breaking off now and then to give a command to the helmsman. All Simon could see was the straining back of the oarsman immediately in front of him, but he found himself caught up in the excitement of the chase.

He reminded himself that he was opposed to whaling on principle, but the principle didn't seem to relate to the occasion. And this, after all, was no factory ship hounding a helpless victim, but a cockleshell of a boat far smaller than its quarry. If the whale proved to be a Moby Dick, and turned on them . . . He scared himself with that thought for a moment, but the frenzied atmosphere was irresistibly contagious. The Vikings were yelling like madmen, and he found himself yelling along with them.

Two had detached themselves from the forward oars and stood on the platform beside Wulfgar, holding harpoons attached to lines. Wulfgar also had a harpoon. Simon could just glimpse him past the shoulder of the oarsman in front, grinning and exultant, his yellow hair streaming out from under his helmet in the wind. He looked like a child at a party.

The squall swept in suddenly from the starboard quarter, stinging them with darts of cold rain, and the sky darkened. It lasted only a matter of minutes before the sun came out again, but there was another following close. For perhaps a quarter of an hour, rain was intermittent, but then it turned into a steady chilling downpour. The cries of the oarsmen grew less enthusiastic, and the rowing rate eased perceptibly.

Not long after, Wulfgar called to them: "We have lost him. This expedition is ill-fated. We will set course for home."

The air of gloom was as pronounced now as the excitement

had been. The two harpooners returned despondently to their seats. Wulfgar, though, was not downcast.

"Our luck will change," he cried. "After the winter feast, we shall take whales by the dozen. Odin will provide for his children. At the winter feast, the eagles will spread their wings, and then we shall live prosperously on Odin's bounty. Now, home!"

That night in the hut, Bos grumbled about the premature ending of the whale hunt. The helmsman in his ship had claimed to have the whale still in view when the chase was called off.

Curtius said: "The rain dampened their spirits. In my ship they were complaining of it, like children. In the imperial Roman army we marched for many long days through rain far heavier, and slaughtered barbarians at the march's end."

"I was surprised they gave up so easily," Simon said, "when they're short of oil and running short of food."

"They talk of their winter feast," Bos said, "when eagles spread their wings. I have seen no eagles here. I said that to them, and they laughed."

"They are children," Curtius insisted. "I like them well enough, but they are children. They laugh for no reason."

Brad said: "It is puzzling. Wulfgar seems very confident Odin is going to take care of them, but I don't see how he expects it to happen."

Bos shook his head. "They can expect nothing from pagan gods."

Curtius said: "I pay my due respects to the gods, as a wise man should, but I would never wait on their aid. The gods, in any case, help those best who help themselves."

"It's not long now to the winter feast," Simon said. "A couple of weeks. It's probably just a morale booster: something to keep them going."

"Children . . ." said Curtius.

There was an increasing mood of anticipation in the village, something like that which Simon remembered from Christmases when he was little. The women spent a good deal of time preparing for the feast. They were very cheerful, with one exception. That was Lundiga, who seemed preoccupied and withdrawn.

Brad commented on it. "She's unhappy about something."

"Do you think so?"

Simon had been hoping the preoccupation might be connected with him. She no longer greeted his compliments with amused smiles, but with worried looks. It might represent progress. He felt there had been a change in her attitude altogether. It would be easier if he could talk to her without having Brad along, but she remained adamant about that.

Brad said: "I'm sure so."

They were on their way to join her. There had been a good fall of snow, and she had said she would take them to a tobogganing slope outside the village.

She was waiting with the toboggan at her parents' hut, and walked quietly beside them as Simon carried it out of the village. She really was very quiet this morning, barely responding to his attempts to strike up conversation; yet he did not feel the silence was a hostile one. She was looking very beautiful, her cheeks pinker than ever in the crisp air.

She led them to a ridge half a mile from the village, overlooking a saucer-shaped hollow. The toboggan was meant for two but would take three. They made several runs, producing a progressively faster track as the snow compacted.

Suddenly Lundiga said she would not go on the next run, and before Brad could say anything, Simon said he would skip it, too. Brad shrugged and got down on the sled, immediately launching himself down the slope. He wound up with a fancy twist at the bottom, scattering a cloud of snow. He started back up with the sled.

Simon said: "You're looking prettier than ever today, Lundiga."

It wasn't a particularly stylish compliment, but his command of Latin did not extend to stylishness, and if it had, Lundiga, speaking only the barbarous Latin of the Vikings, probably wouldn't have appreciated it. He did his best to improve things by gazing earnestly into her eyes, and was disconcerted to find them brimming with tears. He was even more taken aback when she burst into loud sobs. He put a comforting arm round her, and she did not shake it off.

Brad, hauling the toboggan up the last bit of slope, said accusingly: "What have you been doing to her?"

"Nothing."

Brad's look was sceptical.

"No, really, nothing!"

Lundiga detached herself but did not move away. Surveying them through tears, she said: "You must go."

"Go?" Simon stared at her. "Go where?"

"Away from here. From the island."

"But why?"

Simon's acquaintance with the opposite sex was a limited one, but it had taught him that avowals need not always be taken at face value. Go away might mean come closer. He took her hand, and said: "I'm not going anywhere."

She looked at him, then turned to Brad.

"You asked me once about how it was my people came here, and I said I did not know. That was not true, Bradus."

He said: "I wondered at the time. There's always some story or legend, even if it's not very accurate."

"It was because of you Romans. A long time ago—more than thirty generations."

She paused. "My people were part of the empire. We spoke the language of the empire, obeyed the Emperor's commands. But in the northern mountains there were those of our race who had not submitted to the Romans. They had many children and not enough food. They came south, and called on my people to rise against the Romans. Our ancestors joined with them, and together they won a great battle against the Roman army. But the Emperor had other armies. In the next battle, our ancestors were defeated, with great slaughter."

She paused again, and Brad said to Simon in English: "More than thirty generations. That would make it about the time the Viking expeditions started in our world. In this one, the Danes had been Romanized, and Rome itself was still powerful. So if the Norwegians and Swedes moved south, and called on the Romanized Danes to join them . . . It makes sense."

Lundiga said: "I do not understand your words."

In Latin, Brad said: "It doesn't matter. What happened — after your people's army was defeated?"

"Roman soldiers entered our land, pursuing those who had fled. They not only killed men, but tortured and murdered women and children. They burned towns and villages, the people along with the houses."

"Very Roman," Brad commented. "They did the same after Boudicca's revolt. They were always more cruel towards those who had been Romanized. In their eyes it was a special kind of treachery to revolt against Roman rule."

"In one town," Lundiga said, "hearing what the Romans had done in other places, the people took their longships and set sail. There were stories of a land called Thule that lay far off in the great ocean, beyond Britain. They did not know if the stories were true, but chose the perils of the sea rather than the merciless ferocity of the Romans. Four longships sailed, and three were lost. The fourth found safe landing here.

"For many generations my people prospered on this island, and were happy. In the last hundred years it has been harder. We have less of everything: ships, huts, food. And children. The present is dark, the future darker still."

Simon said: "But your people seem cheerful enough. And they talk of good times to come. They say Odin is going to help them, after the winter feast."

She began to cry again.

In a strange, wary voice, Brad said: "Just what is this stuff about Odin, and the winter feast, and the eagles?"

"We have a legend, passed down from the early days. It spoke of hard times to come, very hard, and said they would not pass until Romans came to the island."

"Well," Simon said, "that's all right, isn't it? Here we are."

She stared miserably at them. "The legend said the Romans would come—to be a sacrifice to Odin at the winter feast. After that, Odin will bring good times again."

Simon could not believe what he was hearing. He said: "But the flying eagles . . ."

"I remember now," Brad said. "It's something that's been at the back of my mind, but I didn't make the connection. A very old form of Scandinavian ritual killing. The eagles don't fly: they simply spread their wings. What that means, precisely, is that someone cuts the victims' chests open, and slowly bends the ribs outwards till they look like wings. It was called the bloody eagle."

He looked at Lundiga.

"And we are to be the eagles?"

4

Bos swore, and went on swearing for a long time.

Curtius was incredulous. He demanded: "Are you certain of this?"

"Sure enough," Brad said.

"But what reason would the girl have for telling you? By doing so, she betrays her people."

Bos said impatiently: "There is no problem there. Have you not seen young Simonus here making eyes at her? The Sabine women preferred the Roman husbands who had snatched them to the fathers who had nurtured them. And I think what she said is true. They laughed when I asked about the eagles, and there was something about that laugh I now remember. When I was a child and the Romans took my village, my mother pleaded for my father's life. The centurion laughed like that, before he ran him through."

Curtius's swarthy face had been darkening as Bos spoke. He said: "Did I call them children? They are treacherous curs. Let us go at once and kill them."

"Four of us," Simon said, "against roughly a hundred? I don't like the odds."

"For all their horned helmets and axes," Curtius said contemptuously, "they are more women than warriors. Indeed, I believe their women might fight better."

Brad said: "You could be right about that. Which would make the odds around two hundred to four. Curtius, we have to be sensible. We've had the good luck to be warned in advance. We can take advantage of that."

"Wait till tonight, then," Bos suggested. "They will get drunk in the hall, as they always do. That is the time to fall on them and hack them to pieces."

Curtius nodded reluctantly. "Perhaps I can wait till tonight."

Simon said: "Are you both mad? They'd probably fight better for being drunk. And there are the women, as Brad said. Killing them isn't important, anyway. Getting clear of the island is."

Curtius looked obstinate, but Bos asked: "What do you say we should do?"

"The winter feast," Brad said, "takes place at the full moon. The moon's half full now, so we have time to make preparations. Our best plan obviously is to escape by night in one of the longships. There are things we'll need, like food and water for the voyage. We must choose the right moment."

"How soon?" Bos asked.

"Not right now, certainly. We want a clear night."

The weather had been dull for days, with a sharp east

wind and low cloud. Curtius said: "What if there is no clear night before the feast?"

"Then we'll have to take a chance on getting away in the dark. But it'll be a lot easier with a moon."

"And there's the question," Simon put in, "of when Lundiga can get away."

Curtius scowled at him. "We do not take the girl."

Simon said: "Without her warning us we'd be heading for a nasty death. Of course she's coming."

"She is one of them," Curtius said, "and therefore not to be trusted."

Bos said: "What you say is right, Simonus. But she will be better off here, with her own people."

"Lundiga betrayed her people when she warned us," Brad said, "as Curtius pointed out. If we disappear, they'll be pretty sure it's because we found out what they had planned. And since she's been with Simonus and me so much they're bound to suspect her of telling us. We have to take her."

Curtius shook his head. "I say leave her."

Bos looked troubled. "I like the girl. And she has done us a favour beyond price. If you think she would be in danger . . ."

"Right," Simon said. "That's three to one. Lundiga comes with us."

Curtius said in disgust: "I would still rather go out there now and kill them all."

They spoke to Lundiga next morning. Simon said: "We'll let you know when we've fixed the time for going. The safest way will be for you to slip away and join up with us on the quayside."

She looked at him in surprise. "Oh, no."

"What do you mean—no?"

"I told you because I could not bear that you should be killed. But I could not go away with you. That is not proper."

She spoke with a flat certainty Simon recognized. Surprise was succeeded by exasperation.

"What's proper got to do with it? You *must* get out of here."

Her yellow hair swung with the shake of her head. "I cannot."

Brad took up the argument. "Simonus is right. What would happen if your people knew you'd warned us?"

She said simply: "My father would kill me with his own hands."

"There you are! And they'll know someone told us. They'll guess it was you."

She looked at Brad with unhappy eyes, but said after a moment: "It is not proper."

Simon had a moment of fury. She really was pigheaded to the point of dumbness. He raised his voice.

"It's your *life* we're talking about. You have to come."

"No." Her mother was heading in their direction. "I must go."

Later Simon said: "We'll take her by force if necessary."

"I can see us doing that," Brad said, "—carrying her kicking and screaming down to the longships. At least, I can just about imagine you or Bos trying it. I doubt I could lift her."

"When it came to the point, she might not resist."

"On the other hand, she might, and it would only take one yell to have them on our necks. She sleeps in her parents' hut. How do you feel about getting her out at dead of night, without waking anyone else?"

"We can't just leave her to be slaughtered."

"She may not be. They can never be certain, unless she tells them. And she is Wulfgar's daughter."

"That wouldn't save her—she said so."

"Anyway, they can't be *sure*. We might have overheard something one of the Vikings said. Or figured things out from their laughing when Bos said he'd seen no eagles."

"You don't really believe that."

"I believe we have to face facts. There's no way of taking her except voluntarily, and so far she's determined not to come. We can keep trying to persuade her." He grinned. "You're probably better qualified for that job."

Simon did his best. He worried at first that the change in the weather might come before his persuasive powers had time to take effect, but days of cloud succeeded one another unremittingly, while on the other hand Lundiga seemed to grow stubborner as time went by.

One morning they woke to find a blizzard sweeping in from the west. It snowed all day, and as night came with snow still falling, Simon realized that the invisible moon would be three-quarters full. The moment was approaching when they would have to take their chance without moonlight. And without Lundiga.

Next day the snow had ceased, and the clouds were breaking; patches of sunlight made the whiteness dazzle. Bos and Curtius were jubilant, seeing this as the signal to go. When Simon argued for giving it another day, Curtius said: "Another day may mean another blizzard. It must be tonight."

Brad said: "He is right, you know. We can't afford to wait."

Bos said: "It is true, Simonus. I am sorry for the girl, but she must take her own chances now."

Lundiga was clearing snow from the paths with the rest of the women, but they managed to get her on her own. Simon explained that they would be leaving that night. She listened in silence, leaning on a broad wooden shovel. He spoke urgently, though with no real hope of convincing her. "You must come with us, Lundiga. Please!"

She was silent.

Brad said: "We'd better not stay long talking. It's something that could be remembered tomorrow, and make things trickier for her."

Simon said: "Lundiga . . ."

"It is not proper." She paused. "But there are some things which cannot be denied. I said I could not bear the thought of you being killed, but it was not just that. All my life I have lived among my people and known no others. When you came here, I saw you as outlanders and, worse, as Romans. Even when I smiled at you, I remembered what your ancestors had done to mine. But my heart has changed as I have come to know you better—one of you, in particular."

Her look fastened on Brad. "I have thought about it through many wakeful nights, and I know what I must do because my heart commands it. I cannot bear the thought of losing you, Bradus. Since you must go, I shall go with you."

Before supper that evening Bos slipped away; on a reconnaissance, he said. Brad urged him not to do anything suspicious, a warning which the big man treated with amiable contempt. He turned the point against Brad later when Brad suggested he and Curtius ought to cut down on their drinking after supper, so as to keep clearer heads.

"That really would be suspicious, eh Curtius? Don't worry, lad. A man who has been schooled on wine can outdrink any of these ale swillers and stay cold sober."

When at last they went back to the hut, the night sky was bright with starlight and the incandescence of a moon close to full. They allowed an hour before setting out again, their footsteps crunching on the packed snow. The things they needed for the voyage had been hidden beneath rubbish in one of the abandoned huts. It was not far from there to the chief's hut. From a distance, Bos gave the owl hoot which was the signal to Lundiga.

It sounded exactly like an owl; if she were asleep it would scarcely wake her. And they were committed now; could not wait. Bos hooted again and, after a few moments, turned to them, shaking his head. But at that moment Lundiga slipped out of the shadows.

They had earmarked Wulfgar's own longship for the enterprise. As they made their way down the hill, they could see its dragon head swaying against the moonlit waters of the bay. The noise of their footsteps on the snow seemed very loud, and Simon was glad when they were clear of the village. Despite the cold, he was sweating.

When they were no more than fifty yards from the quay, there was a sudden outburst of wild screeching behind them. Simon glanced back quickly. The din was emanating from the chief's hut, or rather from a figure just outside it: Lundiga's mother.

Even at this distance the sound was shattering; up among

the huts it must have been ear-piercing. Viking men came running out.

Curtius spoke sharply. "Into the boat! I'll cast off."

His voice carried the authority of a Roman centurion, and they did not argue. The quay was a narrow wooden structure, raised on piles and connected with the shore by a rickety causeway. They clattered over it. Lundiga seemed to hesitate, and Bos picked her up as though she were a baby and dropped her into the longship; then he and Simon and Brad followed. Curtius was wrestling with the rope that secured the ship to its mooring pole.

"Axe it!" Bos shouted.

Curtius swung his axe violently. The deck beneath them shuddered from the impact, but the rope failed to part. He swung a second time, and a third. By now the Vikings were charging down the slope and very close.

An end of rope dropped loose on the deck and Bos shouted to Curtius to jump. Simon was in the prow and could see across the quay to the galloping Vikings. One was in advance of the rest: Wulfgar, barefooted and without his helmet but brandishing his axe, bellowing incoherent threats. Curtius too could see him. He uttered a growl which swelled to a roar of anger.

Brad shouted: "You fool, Curtius! Never mind about him. Jump!"

Instead of doing so, Curtius leapt back and stood blocking the causeway. Wulfgar came at him, and they swung their axes. There was a howl of pain from Wulfgar, of triumph from Curtius, and the Viking went down. But as he did, he grappled with the Roman, holding him.

Lundiga gave a great howl of anguish at the sight and made for the side of the ship. Simon grabbed her but could not hold her; it took Bos's strength to prevent her leaping off. The ship was already drifting away: there was a widening gap of water between them and the quay.

They watched helplessly as the pack of Vikings crowded forward and Curtius sank under their assault. For a moment or two he was invisible, but then amazingly rose again out of the melee, his axe arm flailing. A figure toppled from the causeway and splashed into the water. But the rest were all round him, and a couple had got between him and the quay.

Bos said in a low voice: "We can do nothing."

He grabbed an oar and jabbed it hard against the next ship in line: the gap of water widened.

"Man the oars," Bos shouted.

As he took an oar, Simon saw two axe blows strike Curtius simultaneously; he dropped again, and this time there could be no getting up. At least he had got the battle he had been pining for and the death he would have chosen. There was no more time for reflection. Simon concentrated on rowing.

He had wondered whether Lundiga would take advantage of their preoccupation and jump into the water to swim back: there was nothing that could be done about it if she did. But she simply sat staring into the night. The Vikings, on the other hand, were wasting no time; within seconds they were piling into the remaining longships and casting off. Visibility was excellent across the silvery bay; the moon, for which they had waited so impatiently, was an enemy now.

"Pull!" Bos roared. "For your lives . . ."

Heaving on his oar, Simon was aware of the hopelessness of it. There were three of them against dozens in the other two longships. The leading one was closing; within minutes it would be alongside, with Vikings pouring across. He envied Curtius the blood lust which had marked his last few moments; all he himself felt was the icy bite of fear.

The men in the following ships were yelling in anticipation, but suddenly the tone changed. There were cries of bewilderment. Pulling on the oar, Simon thought he noticed something different about the longship nearest to them. Was it lower in the water? And the gap between them—it was no longer narrowing, but widening.

The pursuing dragon's head rose sharply, as though it were a wingless beast trying to fly. The cries changed to a clamour of despair. The head stood right up, for a moment blacking out the moon. Only for a moment; then, with a giant's gurgle, it slid beneath the water.

Astern of it, the second ship was also tilting. Simon said: "How did that happen?"

"I'm not sure," Brad said, "but I think I have an idea."

They had all stopped rowing. He looked across at Bos, whose teeth gleamed in a grin.

"That little reconnaissance you insisted on making . . . it didn't by any chance include coming down to the quay to loosen a timber or two?"

"Leave nothing to chance," Bos said. "It is the first thing a gladiator learns. Otherwise he does not live to learn anything else."

He released his oar and stood up, stretching out a hand. "A fair breeze, and from the right quarter. Let us get that sail up."

Their first intention had been to head for the nearest point on the mainland, but once they were clear of the harbour and in open sea, Bos had another idea. The wind was from the northeast, filling the longship's sail. Brad had said this coast was of great extent: why not aim for a point further south, out of winter's grip?

Brad at first argued against it, but when Simon strongly supported Bos he did not press his objection. Two to one was a clear majority anyway; Lundiga sat huddled and silent, paying little attention to her surroundings. It was understandable that the double shock, of seeing her father struck down in combat and of leaving the small island which was the only place she had known, should have subdued her.

The others, too, once the initial excitement of the escape was over, were hit by the realization of Curtius's death. It was a loss that affected all of them, but especially Bos. Curtius had been closer to him in age, and they had shared more of a common background; although born a barbarian, Bos had been captured and brought south at an early age. What had happened made him more deeply aware of the distance he had travelled from familiar places and people, leaving him bewildered and unhappy. Simon and Brad did their best to cheer him up, but to little effect. Of course, Bos believed they were heading towards their own country, while he was all the time going further away from his.

At least the weather was good; the sun rose out of a calm sea and the wind stayed fair. Rowing was unnecessary, and they closed the shutters over the oar-ports. It would have all been very pleasant, Simon thought, but for the two melancholy ones on their hands. Having had small success with Bos, they turned their attentions to Lundiga. She seemed not to respond at first, and Simon gave up on it. Brad persisted, trying to divert her with talk of the wonderful land of California which was their eventual destination. Lack of response did not seem to bother him; in fact Simon had a feeling he was talking as much for his own satisfaction as hers.

At any rate he went on and on with his account of the wonders of this earthly paradise, and it produced a sudden and unexpected result when Lundiga burst into laughter.

"You are better than our Viking men," she said, "with their stories of the whales they almost caught. Go on, little Bradus. I like hearing you talk."

When he protested that he was giving a true account, she shook her fur-hatted head, smiling, and said it was no shame to tell tall tales: all men did. The hat completed an outfit which had quite transformed her appearance. She had bound her breasts under the shapeless coat of skins they all wore, and had the look more of a husky boy than a girl. In the middle of the day, with the sun quite warm, Simon tried to persuade her at least to take the hat off, but she refused.

"It is not proper."

Simon was tired of hearing the phrase, but he was beginning to understand the ironclad prejudices of the Viking women. Her infatuation with Brad might have persuaded her to come away with them, but that did not mean she was willing to relax tribal conventions. Quite the reverse, probably. Her amusement over Brad's stories of California was a part of that outlook. She came from long generations of women who had cared for their drunken feckless menfolk with a mixture of affection and contempt.

They kept a course of south-southwest, and were reasonably confident of holding to it. The sun rose and set in the right places, and by night the polestar was properly fixed in the starboard stern quarter. Bos's guess was that they were covering something like two hundred miles in twenty-four hours. On the morning of the third day, the breeze had moderated and lost the last of its chilly edge. Simon saw a flash of distant silver which might have been a flying fish.

They agreed they had come far enough south, and towards the end of the morning altered course to sail west.

Land—Brad guessed South Carolina—became visible in late afternoon, a dark edge to the sun-speckled horizon which gradually broadened. They entered a flattened arc of bay, stretching limitlessly north and south. Beyond the beach there was scrub, with wooded land further back. Bos had the tiller and steered straight for the shore. They ground to a shuddering halt in shallow water just as the sun's rim touched the tops of the trees.

They remained with the ship that night and set off inland next morning. They had landed at high tide and the longship was beached above the water level, which was reassuring. If the present exploration proved unpromising, it might be possible to retrace their steps and use it to find a different landfall.

To start with, the going was easy, over fairly level ground covered with coarse grass and bushes. They had their first check after about three hours, when they reached a river. As it was flowing only slightly south of west, it made sense to follow it. After a couple of miles, though, it abruptly changed direction to due south. Simon was for staying with it, and Bos, who had perked up remarkably since they got back on dry land, agreed. But Brad pointed out that it seemed shallow enough to wade, and insisted on crossing. It was important not to get sidetracked from their westerly bearing.

"Why?" Simon asked. "Because of California? What's wrong with Florida? That's meant to be an earthly paradise, too, isn't it? Don't those golden fruits as big as a man's head you were telling Lundiga about grow there, too? And it's a whole lot nearer."

Brad said: "When you have a plan, it's important to stick to it. Otherwise you're likely to end up aimlessly wandering." He spoke almost peevishly.

Lundiga immediately lent him her support, at the same time patting him indulgently. She called him "little Bradus" again, which made him wince. Ordinarily that would have amused Simon, but he was too incensed by Brad's stubbornness.

He said: "Look, we've covered about six miles from the coast. That leaves two thousand nine hundred and ninety-four to go, give or take a few hundred. The whole business is crazy."

Unexpectedly, Bos clapped a hand on Brad's shoulder. "It is proper to love the land of one's birth." His face was briefly gloomy again. "My own is lost beyond recovery, but it is right for Bradus to seek his. We will go west with him."

Simon said in English: "He's got that a bit wrong, hasn't he? We were a lot nearer the land of your birth among the Algonquians."

Brad did not bother to reply, and Simon decided to let it go. Basically it didn't matter a lot which way they went. He would have preferred staying dry, but sooner or later they were going to have rivers to cross: they would find neither bridges nor ferryman in these parts.

The river was generally less than waist-high, even in the middle, but Simon managed to find a hole which submerged him up to his neck. The wet skins clung heavily as they continued their trek, reviving his annoyance with Brad. It was a point, though, which lost its importance within the hour when the sky, which had been rapidly clouding from the west, opened to soak them all.

They settled for the night under a broad-branched evergreen which promised a degree of protection against the persisting rain. It fell some way short of providing a complete shield, and they were heavily dripped on as they chewed dried fish and stale cornbread. But at least it was rain, not snow, and the temperature was well above freezing. Tired from the day's trudging, they slept heavily.

On the third day they came out of woodland into a patch of what had plainly been cultivated land, though it was in the process of reverting to wilderness. That indicated an Indian village nearby, and they reached it soon after. Food was beginning to run short and they had not found anything edible since coming ashore: presumably there were fish in the rivers, but they had no means of catching them. They decided to take a chance on their reception from the Indians.

The village consisted of about a score of small huts, which differed from the Algonquian tepees in being rectangular in shape. They were supported by poles at the corners and thatched with large dried leaves. A stream ran close by and small children, two girls and a boy, were playing by it; they looked at the newcomers with curiosity but without alarm. Adults appeared from the huts. The men wore coats of some kind of cloth, and the women dresses, or rather lengths of cloth with holes cut for the head and arms. Simon was more concerned with the expression on their faces, and he was relieved to see they looked amiable.

They proved to be not just amiable, but actively hospitable. Food was offered before they asked—tortillas with spicy fillings and a sweet maize gruel served in small gourds. The Indians chattered round them while they ate, showing particular interest in Bos's beard. These men, like the northern Indians, were facially practically hairless. The small dogs that sniffed around their feet were hairless, too.

They were housed for the night in a hut which showed signs of recent use; Simon guessed the usual occupants had doubled up elsewhere to make room for them. In the morning they were given rations for the onward journey. Late on the day after that, they found another village, and thereafter were never more than two or three days' travel from human habitation.

These Indians were quite different from the unsmiling Algonquians. At one village, where they arrived soaked from a rainstorm, a complete change of clothes was provided for them. The cloth was woven from bark fibres but far more comfortable than the skins they had been wearing and which, with the temperature so much higher, they were glad to abandon.

Lundiga, however, insisted on retaining both her fur hat and her boyish disguise. That helped him, Simon felt, in adjusting to her transparent devotion to Brad; she just didn't look like a girl. Another factor was that the devotion had a protective, in fact patronizing, aspect which was funny to observe, and which Brad found increasingly infuriating. In the end, when she had addressed him as "little Bradus" once too often, his resentment boiled over and he abused her roundly. She looked hurt for a moment, and Bos, who had developed a sort of fatherly fondness for her, rebuked Brad for his unkindness, reminding him what they all owed to her.

"And she is a nice girl, Bradus. You are lucky that such a nice girl is fond of you."

Brad looked sullen. Simon thought it best to conceal his amusement. Lundiga rapidly recovered, and continued with her attentions. No, Simon decided, he was well out of that one.

They had no reason for keeping track of time, and he had no notion how long their leisurely progress had continued. Weeks certainly. They had grown accustomed to it: one day and one village was very like the next.

Then, on a morning spitting rain, they came over a wooded crest to see flat country ahead. It was bare rock for the most part, studded with rocky protuberances. But there was something else that caught the eye and brought a shiver of excitement to the mind. About a mile away the landscape was divided by a narrow band that ran roughly east-west and very straight. Simon stared in amazement. There was no possibility of its being a natural phenomenon: what they were looking at was a highway.

5

THEY RAN THE FINAL hundred yards. The road was about fifteen feet wide, with a base of large, shaped stones and a surface of compacted chippings.

"This was not made by Romans," Bos said. "The workmanship is not good enough."

There was disappointment in his voice. However impossible the notion of coming on a Roman road in this wild land, seeing a man-made highway after all this time of trackless woods must have been like a glimpse of home.

Brad said: "No, certainly not Roman. It has to be Incan. They were the only people in America who built a road system."

"But weren't the Incas in South America?" Simon asked.

"Yes. They were centred around Peru, and the furthest north they reached was Ecuador. But that was a world where the Spaniards clobbered them in the early sixteenth century. A lot can happen in four hundred years. Things may have stayed static in Europe, but it looks as though they got moving over here. There's one puzzling thing, though."

"What?"

"The Spaniards destroyed two American cultures, not one. A little while before Pizarro conquered the Incas, Cortes was wiping out the Aztecs. And the Aztecs were in Mexico, which is a lot nearer. These two empires never actually made contact."

"In our world, they didn't," Simon said. "They must have done here, and I suppose they fought and the Incas won."

He could see Brad was ready for a prolonged speculation on the subject, which he felt he could do without.

He said: "Anyway, what matters is that this is a road we're standing on, and if it's not quite up to Roman standards, it's not bad either. So at any moment we might see a stagecoach rolling towards us with four vacant seats."

"No chance."

"Well, maybe not with empty seats. Maybe not a stagecoach even. I'd settle for a horse and cart."

"Not even that. There were no horses in the Americas till the Spaniards introduced them, after Columbus. And no wheels, for that matter. Although they had wheeled toys, for some reason they never thought of using wheels for transportation."

"But they did have roads? Just for pedestrians?"

"Sure. The Romans basically built their roads for pedestrians—for the Roman infantry. Good roads mean you can move troops around fast."

"Well, we can take advantage of it," Simon said. "It's pointing west, too. California, here we come."

*

They set out again, making very much better progress. The earlier rain had given way to sunshine, and a breeze which dried their clothes on them. Their spirits were high. Bos sang a gladiator's song, and Simon joined in with him. It was Lundiga, walking, as she usually did, directly behind Brad, who noticed something unusual. She said: "Listen . . ."

As soon as he stopped singing, Simon heard it: a faint rhythmic drumming behind them. Turning, he saw dots on the road, about three-quarters of a mile back. Although details could not be made out at that distance, he saw there were three of them and that they were mounted.

To Brad he said: "So there aren't any horses in this continent?"

Brad studied the figures, frowning. He said at last: "They're not horses."

"Don't be silly. What else can . . . ?" He broke off. The animals, he saw, walked with a strange swaying motion, and they had small heads set on long high necks.

Brad said: "It's known they were used as baggage animals, so I guess there's no reason someone shouldn't have thought to put a saddle on them. Those are llamas."

They waited by the roadside while the riders caught up with them. They were far more elaborately and colourfully dressed than the village Indians they had become accustomed to. The lead figure was particularly splendid; he had an ankle-length cloak of bright scarlet with swirls of green, while the other two were in darker red, striped with black. These also wore helmets, but the one in front had a framelike contraption on the back of his head which sprouted vivid sprays of feathers. The faces of all three were dark and insolent.

When they were abreast, Bos called out a greeting. Since it was in Latin, they could scarcely have been expected to understand him, but the travellers did not even turn their heads. The helmeted couple had belts over their cloaks, with nasty-looking daggers tucked in them; they were probably a bodyguard to the third. Simon was glad Bos did not persist in trying to attract their attention; they looked pretty unpleasant.

As they rode away, Bos spat on the ground.

"A friendly lot."

"That must be the upper class," Brad commented. "They obviously regard peasants like us as beneath notice."

Simon said: "I wonder which way to the nearest town? Do you think they're starting their journey or finishing it?"

"They could be halfway through," Brad said. "But they're going in the right direction, so we might as well follow."

At first it looked like the peak of a distant mountain; later its symmetry identified it as a tower. Other buildings subsequently became visible crowding about its base: a city lay ahead. As they went on, there were cultivated fields on either side of the highway, and they met more traffic, both llama-riders and pedestrians; the latter were much more simply dressed, not very different from the village Indians.

Long low buildings were dotted among the fields and plantations, and peasant shacks beside the road increased in number until the road turned into a street. They passed a big open space where stalls had been set up, selling a variety of goods. Not long after that, the shacks started to give way to more substantial stone buildings. Simon noticed that these, like the shacks, had no doors as such, but the curtains that covered the doorways were of ornate beadwork instead of simple reeds.

The road they were on was crossed by others, and they passed through squares where four roads met. Eventually they reached a vast plaza lined with buildings. They were impressive, but looked insignificant when viewed against what stood in the centre of the plaza. It was the tower they had seen from far out on the plain.

They halted, staring, and Lundiga gave a small cry of astonishment. Bos, who had seen the temples and palaces of Rome as well as Londinium, was reduced to silence. Even for Brad and Simon, with memories of London and New York, it was awe-inspiring.

It was square-based, and built in stepped blocks to form a pyramid that rose at least a hundred and fifty feet from the ground. Each block was five or six feet high, making scaling difficult if not impossible, but a ramp was built into the side facing them, giving access to the top. The ramp had stone steps, which a man in a white and purple robe was climbing. There was a pavilion at the apex, its walls brightly coloured in contrast with the dazzling white stucco of the rest of the pyramid.

"A temple?" Bos asked.

"Yes." Brad was staring at it with a puzzled look.

Bos said: "I wonder what gods they worship there?"

The Incas, Simon recalled, had been heavily into human sacrifice. He said: "Not very nice ones."

Brad said: "I got it wrong."

"Not like you," Simon said. "What are we talking about, by the way?"

"Bos's question about the gods they worship . . . the Incas took their sun god with them wherever they conquered:

they allowed their subjects a certain amount of freedom of choice, but not in religion. But that's not a sun god temple. See those carvings on either side of the ramp? The one on the right's the God of War. The other is the Feathered Snake, otherwise Tlaloc, the Rain God.

"The two empires met, all right, and fought it out. I thought the Incas must have won, because of the road system. But it's very easy, and not unusual, to pick up technical know-how from the peoples you subdue. What you don't take on is religion: you impose your own. That temple is dedicated to Aztec gods, which means it was the Aztecs who won out. This is an Aztec city."

"They practised human sacrifice, too, didn't they?"

Brad nodded. "Even more than the Incas."

Simon looked up at the pyramid. It was awesome, beautiful in its way; but hideous at the same time. He said: "Let's move on."

No one argued.

In marked contrast to their experience among the Indian villages, they were offered no hospitality or help in the city, which they learned was called Palzibil. Its population consisted of three classes of people: the rich, the poor, and the slaves of the rich. The gulf between rich and poor was very great.

The city was still growing, or at least its stone-built inner area was expanding out into the part occupied by shacks, and they managed to find work as labourers in the construction industry. They were paid in cocoa beans tied up in small bags that held varying quantities. This was the general basic currency, though at higher levels small silver ingots and duck or turkey quills packed with gold dust were in use.

Their daily wage enabled them to buy food, but did not leave much over.

They were not the only foreigners in the city: there was a considerable number of Indians who had left their villages for one reason or another and made their way here. These mostly slept in the open, and Simon and the others found themselves obliged to follow suit. Many of the larger buildings had external porticoes, and they were able to sleep under them, obtaining protection against rain at least. It was necessary to be up and away early, though, to avoid being kicked into a gutter by the servants of the owners of the house.

After a week, Brad proposed moving on. "This is a dead-end situation. We're not even earning enough money to buy new clothes when these wear out. And you can bet your life no one here is going to give us any."

"It's early days," Simon said.

"What difference does that make? Early, middle or late, we're still going to be on the bread line. It's a rigid setup. The rich are very rich and the poor are very poor, and they don't change places. There's no ladder of success in Aztec society."

"Some things are not so bad," Bos said. "They do not have wine, but that liquor they sell in the market is very cheap." He shook his head in reminiscence. "And fiery."

"I still think we ought to move on," Brad said.

It was the midday break from work, and they were sitting in bright sunshine, their backs against the wall they had been building.

Lundiga, beside Brad, said: "No one bothers us. We get enough to eat. We do not know what it will be like in another place."

"I've told you—much better than this."

"It is warmer here than it was on the island," Lundiga said, "and there is summer yet to come. We are in no hurry." She stroked his cheek, making him pull away in irritation. "Do not worry, little Bradus. We will go with you to your wonderful land of California."

"But not just yet," Simon said. "It's three to one again, buddy, but this time against you."

Life in fact was not all that unpleasant, even for the poor. The work they did was not too arduous. They had a reasonable amount of free time, and there was plenty to see. They steered clear of the frequent religious processions, but there were other entertainments. Some of the buildings were theatres, with wooden benches in tiers above a central stage. There was no admission charge, but the working classes were confined to the cramped upper benches. The lower rows, wider and improved by the addition of gaudy cushions, were reserved for the well-to-do, who did not pay for admission, either, but who tossed things—cloths, feathers, shells, bags of cocoa beans, occasionally silver—to the entertainers at the end of the show.

Additionally there were the ball games, which took place in a large building containing four rectangular courts. A stone ring projected from one side of each court, some fifteen feet above the ground. The ring was approximately four feet across, its internal diameter about half that.

The games were played by two teams of four players, who wore short coats and a lot of padding underneath. With good reason—the proceedings were fast, furious, and liable to cause injury. The players carried what looked like sawed-off versions of lacrosse sticks, and used the pockets at the end of the sticks to catch and subsequently to hurl a small hard rubber ball. The object was to get the ball through the ring, but this was not at all easy; before that happened the ball bounced murderously fast from wall to wall of the court, not infrequently felling one of the participants.

The games were divided into three periods with short breaks between them. The winning side was rewarded, like the entertainers in the theatre, from the lower benches of the tiered seating area.

The Aztecs were fanatically enthusiastic about the sport. Apart from the official contests, scratch games were played everywhere in the streets: in a number of places ramshackle courts had been constructed, and wherever two walls formed an intersection, there were likely to be children hammering a ball against them. Bos became interested first and succeeded in interesting the others. You could buy a stick in the market for one of the smallest bags of beans and, as Brad agreed, it passed the time.

They had begun to get a smattering of the Aztec language, with Brad as usual picking it up the fastest. The humbler Aztecs were reasonably sociable, and some of the Indians now living in the city were Algonquian-speaking and could help interpret.

One day they were resting after a game, munching tortillas they had bought from a street vendor, when Brad said: "I suppose it's not so bad here."

"That," Simon said, "is what we've been telling *you*."

"Put it this way—not bad, but it could be a lot nicer if we were better off financially."

"So dream on. You said it yourself: no ladder of success in Aztec society."

"I was talking about people on a daily wage."

"Well?"

"No ladders, I agree, but what about a springboard? Dancers and musicians don't collect a little bag of beans: they get something worthwhile thrown to them. That juggler we saw last night has six slaves carrying him to the theatre in a litter."

"What do you suggest we do—form a pop group?"

Simon said that in English. Bos and Lundiga were used to their habit of switching into the strange tongue, which they assumed was the language of their homeland in the west.

Brad shook his head. "I don't think the Aztecs are quite ready for rock 'n' roll. Pity. Four's a good number for a group." He paused. "It would also make up a team for the ball game."

"That's even more ridiculous. Every Aztec in the city, from the age of three onwards, would like to get into that. We wouldn't get to first base."

"First base? You're in the wrong ball game. Though in fact it's an interesting line to follow. You know some of the little kids play with their hands instead of using sticks? The original game was a form of handball, and on our side of the fireball, there's no record of it being played any other way. Here it changed, most likely as a result of expansion northwards bringing them into contact with the Indians who played lacrosse. They must have picked up the notion of using sticks from them."

"So what?"

"You've seen the technique of the game. You have to capture the ball in the pocket, hold it, and then sling it at the ring. It requires a lot of skill."

"I agree," Simon said. "Rather more than we've got or are likely to develop."

"But if instead of lacrosse sticks you used something more like a tennis racket . . . you'd get greater impact and a much better control of direction."

"I don't see . . ."

"If we were to modify the sticks—tighten up the leather strips so they formed a flat, resilient surface rather than a pocket . . ."

"They'd never let us use them."

"Why wouldn't they? Someone had the bright idea, maybe a couple of hundred years ago, of switching from handball, and he wasn't disqualified. It made the game faster, and I guess the Aztecs appreciated that. This would make it faster still."

Simon shook his head. "I can't believe we'd get away with it."

"I've been talking to Strong Feather."

Strong Feather was an Algonquian-speaking Indian who had lived in the city for some years and was a valuable source of information on local customs.

Brad went on: "The year's big games take place six weeks from now; they're tied up with some special religious festival, of course. A week before that there's a sort of open qualifying contest, in which new teams slug it out for a place in the main games. We could try out our version of the sticks in that."

"We wouldn't be allowed to."

"What do we have to lose?"

The question, Simon realized, was unanswerable; and anyway it might be fun. Beside him, Bos was snoozing. Simon prodded him with a toe. "Wake up, Bos."

"I am tired—tired of listening to you gabble in that ugly tongue of yours."

"Well, you can start listening in Latin. Bradus has had an idea."

Modifying the sticks did not prove as easy as Brad had anticipated. He came up with a racket that was roughly triangular in shape and small in playing area; moreover, because the wooden surround was not complete, it lacked tautness and consequently was not very resilient. He tried to bend the end round to eliminate the gap, but the wood was much thicker and less yielding than the small saplings they had used in making snowshoes, and he had to abandon the attempt. It was a poor affair altogether. He and Simon tried hitting a ball with it but the results were uninspiring; it seemed no more likely to produce an accurate shot than the original sticks.

"The shape's wrong," Simon said, "and it's too small. It would be like trying to play lawn tennis with a table tennis bat."

Brad stared despondently at the fruit of his labours. "Ah well. One more good idea for the discard pile."

Bos, who had been whittling a piece of wood, strolled over. He asked what they had been doing. When Simon outlined the problem, he said critically: "You need a more curved stick."

"Sure," Simon said. "A branch that curves right round in a circle. There must be thousands of them."

The sticks were made from branches of pecan trees which grew in plantations on the outskirts of the city and were selected for the natural curvature to which the small leather pouch could be fitted. Bos picked up the stick and studied it. "We can bend this."

Brad said: "I suppose *you* might just be able to, but how do you keep it bent?"

"In the same manner that coopers make staves for barrels. With steam."

Brad stared at him. "I'm an idiot. And you're a genius, Bos. Of course!"

Once his interest was captured, Bos took over operations. There was a communal washing place, where, on payment of a small bag of cocoa beans, people could take their clothes to wash in huge vats of bubbling water. They took the sticks, held them in the steam over the vats and Bos's powerful muscles did the rest. It was a long and arduous procedure, but it worked.

The result was scarcely elegant but produced a stick whose end curved round to enclose an oval space about eighteen inches long and half that across. They grooved the sides at half-inch intervals and fitted leather strips horizontally, then added cross strips to complete the grid. Bos handed the completed racket to Simon, who swung it experimentally.

"It wouldn't do for Wimbledon, but it's a big improvement on the other. Throw me a ball, Brad."

Brad tossed him a ball, and Simon hit it hard with the intention of bouncing it against the high stone wall of the washing place. But he got too far under it and it soared up and over the wall.

"You find the ball," Brad said, "or else buy a new one. But I guess we can say we're in business."

They found a good place to practise. Some of the bigger buildings were unoccupied because their owners had gone out to their ranches in the country, and though a patrol checked to ensure squatters didn't move in, this happened at set hours, and they were able to work out the timetable. Once the patrol had passed, it was easy to get inside. They picked a room whose dimensions were reasonably close to those of the ball court and hung up a wooden ring. Then they got down to playing.

It was fun, but also exhausting. Eventually Simon suggested they had done enough for one day. Brad disagreed. "Five weeks isn't long to go from amateur to top pro. I say keep playing."

He got Bos's vote and, even more enthusiastically, Lundiga's. Nor was this, Simon realized, just her customary habit of supporting whatever her little Bradus proposed; she was really hooked on the game. She had a surprisingly good eye and considerable strength of arm—one of her angled shots, ricocheting unexpectedly, almost knocked Simon out when he failed to get out of the way. She was a somewhat comic sight, swinging her racket with the fur hat firmly planted on her head, and Brad again suggested she take it off: there was no one to see her, apart from them.

Her chin jutted firmly. "It is not proper."

They practised each day until the room's high windows no longer gave them enough light to see by. At the beginning, their muscles ached abominably, but gradually they toughened up. The standard of play improved, too; whereas originally it had been an achievement to get the ball through the ring a couple of times in the course of an evening, they began to score more regularly.

There was a ball game three weeks after they started, and they went along to watch.

Bos said: "We are not good enough."

"No," Brad agreed. "I suppose they're about three times better than we are. When we started, it would have been thirty times better. We need more practice."

The city began to fill with people from outside, a week

before the tryout games. They watched from across the street as a convoy of servants with pack llamas arrived at the house they had been using, and started making it ready for their masters.

Bos said: "Shall we look for another? There are houses still empty."

Simon shook his head. "Not worth it."

Brad said reluctantly: "No. They'll all be filling up now."

Lundiga said: "There is a ruin where the children play ball. We could go there."

"The moment we do," Simon said, "everyone will know about the new sticks."

"Would that matter?" Brad asked. He considered it. "I guess you're right. The element of surprise is probably worth more than the extra practice."

That night Simon was awakened from an exhausted sleep to see Brad's figure silhouetted against bright moonlight. The first moment of consciousness had the curious effect of obliterating from his memory everything that had happened since the fireball. He thought he was at home in Surrey and could not understand why his American cousin was squatting beside him, nor why they were not in their beds. Memory came back with a bang, and brought with it a fierce hunger for all the things he had lost—a soft bed, his portable radio ready to switch on, his grandmother's voice calling him to a bacon and egg breakfast . . . He said resentfully: "What is it?"

"A clear night is what," Brad said, "which we can have to ourselves. We can get more practice in."

6

THE DAY BEGAN with a procession that wound its way through the streets of the city towards the temple. The following mob stretched more than half a mile. Lundiga suggested they might go along to see what happened, but Bos opposed it.

"I want no part in pagan doings."

"It's not just the pagan bit," Brad said. "Strong Feather told me what happens. The priests go up to that pavilion at the top, taking a young girl with them. They say their prayers to the two gods; then four attendants hold the girl's legs and arms while the Chief Priest slashes her breast, plunges his hand in, and pulls out her heart. Apparently it's important that it should still be throbbing when it's presented to the gods. After that they roll the body down the side of the pyramid, and then it's flayed, and another priest dances around wearing the skin. I don't think we want to watch that."

Although Lundiga did not argue, Simon was not entirely sure she agreed. He thought of the Viking ceremony of the bloody eagle and wondered whether she would not have been a cheerful and interested spectator of the proceedings at the winter feast, but for taking a fancy to Brad. He had now come to think of her entirely as a companion, and on the whole a good one, but he felt there was a strong streak of the barbarian not far below her genial surface.

"What we can do," Brad suggested, "is head over to the ball court while they're having their nasty fun. After the ceremony, there's sure to be a wild rush to get in line. The contest's limited to thirty-two teams, and at least twice that will want to take part."

They had a long wait in the narrow street adjoining the ball courts before the flood of humanity poured towards them. They were yelling and waving sticks, and Simon wondered if they might be tempted to attack them for pre-empting the number one spot next to the door; but the first four came to a triumphant halt beside them, and the remainder soon sorted themselves out behind.

What conflict there was took place much further down the street, where the question of being team thirty-two or thirty-three was in doubt. There was violent scuffling and blows were exchanged; in the end, one of the contending teams yielded, with one member being carried away by the rest, apparently unconscious. There followed a period of surprisingly patient waiting. Patient, but not quiet; they chattered and sang, and tortilla vendors did a brisk trade in sustaining them against the exertions ahead.

The procedure for the contest was straightforward. The two teams first in line played against one another, and the third and fourth, and so on until sixteen clashes had resulted in sixteen winners. This was repeated twice, leaving four survivors out of the thirty-two.

At this stage the knock-out system was replaced by one in which each team played the other three. A point was awarded for a win, and the members of the team with most points were given the belts which qualified them to play in the main games. A tie on points would be settled by a play-off.

The preliminary rounds were decided on a first ring wins basis. Their opponents in the initial game were a young team who were quick on their feet (which accounted for their being second in line) but not outstandingly skilful otherwise. After a few minutes Lundiga picked up a ball sidewalled to her by Brad and drove it cleanly through the ring. The crowd cheered as their opponents walked despondently off the court.

They got no material reward for their victory; it was the habit of the rich to arrive late, and the lower rows of seats were empty. There were plenty of people in the poorer seats, though. These showed considerable interest both in Bos's beard and Lundiga's hat, calling out wisecracks in Aztec and accompanying them with howls of laughter.

Their second entry to the court gained them a special roar of welcome; they had become local favourites. This game lasted longer, but only because they had several near misses, hitting the edge of the ring, before Simon thumped home a pass from Brad.

The last game before the final play-off was another quick one, and once more Lundiga scored the winning shot. By now some of the lower seats were occupied, and a few small silver ingots were tossed to them. They went back cheerfully to the long low-ceilinged area between the courts where players rested between games. It was a lot emptier since the majority had been eliminated.

Brad counted the takings. "It doesn't make us rich, but it's a start. Better than beans."

"So far it's been easy," Simon said.

"So far. We shouldn't get overconfident."

"The important thing is that we got away with using the rackets. What did that official say when he called you over and looked at yours?"

"I couldn't follow. He didn't stop us from using them. That's what matters."

"We can beat them all," Bos said happily. He patted Lundiga's right arm. "Lundiga is playing very well."

Lundiga stretched, and announced: "I'm hungry." Her appetite had always been healthy, but since the period of strenuous exercise had started, her capacity for eating had outstripped even that of Bos. "Is there a tortilla seller outside?"

Only one court was used for the second session. Every seat was taken, and the centre front row in particular had turned into an eye-wrenching kaleidoscope of colours. That was where friends and relations of the governor sat, on either side of his elaborately carved pew. A group of priests robed in purple and white sat behind him, and directly beneath was the judges' box, with the two officials who presided over the games, timing them by means of a smouldering twine knotted at regular intervals.

There was a small area where players could sit and watch, and the Romans weighed up the opposition from there. Two of the surviving teams had players who were around their age (excluding Bos), but the third team was the one which had fought for and won the last place in the line. Its members were two or three years older.

This gave them a physical advantage which they were far from reluctant to use. Simon nicknamed them the Gorillas. Striking an opponent deliberately with a stick was not permitted, though it happened accidentally more often than was probable, and punching, kicking, and similar assaults were also banned. Body checking, on the other hand, was in order, whether or not the opponent was playing the ball, and was indulged in with gusto.

Having been drawn to play second, they were able to watch the Gorillas in action. Their shooting was not particularly good and they had only scored two rings before time was called, but their opponents were scarcely permitted to get a shot in, being flattened every time they went for the ball. At the end, two of them were limping pitifully.

There was a round of applause for Bos and Lundiga when they went on court. They had little trouble in the first game, scoring four rings (three by Lundiga) without reply. They stayed on court to play the team the Gorillas had beaten, and that was easier still. Their opponents were psychologically as well as physically battered—one could barely hobble —and got in only a few hopeless shots. Lundiga got four rings out of seven this time, and a frenzy of cheers at the end.

In the next game, the Gorillas hammered the second team of youngsters as they had the first. Their opponents scored a ring right at the beginning, which infuriated them. They abandoned serious pursuit of the ball while they slammed into their challengers, and subsequently they were able to take more or less unopposed potshots at the ring. They scored three, and missed ten times as many.

"They're tough," Brad said. He looked at Bos. "Think you can handle them?"

Bos rubbed his hands together. "I can handle them."

The excitement of the crowd was at fever pitch; they howled with joy at the sight of Lundiga and Bos. To the Gorillas they displayed an equivalent hostility, hurling imprecations as they came on court. It was nice to be favourites, Simon thought, but it didn't remove his apprehension about what lay ahead.

The apprehension was justified in the first minute. Brad had angled a ball high off a wall intersection; Simon was standing in a position to receive it, with an outside chance of a ring. He was concentrating on the ball rather than watching his back, and in the instant of swinging his racket, a brawny figure rammed into him and sent him sprawling. He hit the stone floor of the court with a thump that drove the breath from his lungs.

A little later, after similarly putting Brad down, the Gorillas had a shooting chance. It missed, and so did their second, but the third went through the ring. Limping towards Bos, Simon said: "They really are tough."

"Not tough enough," Bos said grimly.

The major part of the damage was being done by the Gorillas' leader, a scarred and broken-nosed bruiser. Bos disregarded the ball and stalked him. When he caught him, he hit him with his full two hundred pounds. The Gorilla went down. One of his companions bounced Lundiga, but Bos was on to him immediately, smacking him against the wall. The ball came loose to Brad, who hit it sweetly through the ring.

From that point, they had their measure, and Lundiga and Simon both scored. The Gorillas, more through luck than accuracy, got a second, but when one of the presiding officials dropped his scarf to signal the end, the score was 5–2.

This time they collected quite a bit more silver and even a couple of quills of gold dust. They were also presented with the gold-trimmed leather belts which qualified them to play in the big games. Afterwards they treated themselves to sweet maize cakes topped with cocoa cream, previously an unaffordable luxury.

"A nice change from bread," Brad said. "In fact, I believe we can say we're finally off the bread line."

"No more humping stone blocks," Simon said.

"Yes," Lundiga said. "I am glad. It was all right for Bos and for you, Simonus; but Bradus should not have to do such work."

All right for her, too, Simon thought; she was at least as strong as he was.

Brad, who was learning to switch off from that sort of remark, said with satisfaction: "And the big games next week."

Bos nodded. "Good."

"More loot," said Simon.

"I don't see why we shouldn't win a game or two," Brad said, "even against the big boys. On the other hand . . ."

"What?"

"The team that wins the final really makes it rich. They usually retire from playing after it."

"We're doing fine," Simon said. "Let's not get too ambitious."

"Why not?" Bos asked.

Simon gingerly fingered a huge bruise on his thigh; various bits of his anatomy were starting to ache quite badly.

He said: "Just because we brought down the Roman empire doesn't mean we're kings of the ball game."

"What do we have to lose?" Brad asked.

Lundiga said tenderly: "I agree with Bradus."

Simon touched another bruise and winced. "Well, that's a surprise."

The following days passed quickly. They rented a house and converted one room into a ball court where they practised assiduously. Simon, who did not share the optimism over the possibility of winning the jackpot, was less keen but went along with the others.

Life was certainly easier. They ate better and were able to buy better clothes, and it was pleasanter sleeping in beds than on the streets. And it was not unpleasant to be recognized and cheered by people who had seen them play, though as far as Simon was concerned, that only happened when he was in the company of Bos or Lundiga.

A couple of days before the games, Strong Feather turned up. He ate cakes and drank chocolate with them, and subsequently Brad and he became involved in a long discussion in Algonquian which Simon could not follow. He picked up one phrase which roughly meant "Win good, lose bad," which struck him as a blinding glimpse of the obvious. Afterwards, though, Brad seemed subdued, and he cut practice short that evening. Simon awoke in the night, and was aware that Brad was awake, too, and restless. By the next day, however, Brad appeared to have recovered his spirits and had them hammering the ball about till Simon felt ready to drop.

The imminence of the games was getting to them. There was bickering about points of play which even extended to

Bos and Lundiga, between whom friction was rare. The cantankerousness continued after they had finished playing, and in the end Simon went for a walk, not for the exercise but to have a change of atmosphere.

On his return he sought Brad out, and said abruptly: "I've seen Strong Feather."

Brad looked up. "Yes?"

"I can understand him when he speaks really slow. We talked about the games."

Brad looked towards the others. Bos was whittling a crucifix and Lundiga was preparing supper. "What about the games?" As Simon opened his mouth to answer, Brad added: "In English—please."

"All right. He confirmed what you said, about the winners of the final in the games being loaded with riches. But he told you something about the losers in that game, didn't he—which you didn't pass on? They qualify for something too: being ritually sacrificed!"

Brad said calmly: "Yes. He says it's the climax of the week's religious ceremonies. The priests cut their hearts out and offer them to the gods."

"So you did know!" Simon stared at him. "I didn't really believe it. What kind of a nut are you?" Brad didn't answer. "And what kind of nuts are the Aztecs, buying a deal like that?"

Brad shrugged. "Religious nuts. It fits in with their beliefs. Winning the games is the greatest thing in the world as far as an Aztec is concerned. As they see it it's right that something as glorious as that should have a grim reverse side. They're more than willing to take their chances. It's the will of the gods, anyway."

"It may fit in with their beliefs. It's no part of mine. As far as I'm concerned, that settles things. There's nothing I want badly enough to risk having my chest excavated by a sacrificial knife."

"I was a bit depressed myself when Strong Feather told me. The prospect doesn't exactly grab me either. But when I thought about it I realized there's something that makes a difference. We're not Aztecs."

"Are you trying to tell me foreigners get excused sacrifice?"

"No. I mean Aztecs are bound by their religious commitments, and we're not. We don't have to go as far as the final. These games are a straight knock-out competition for sixteen teams, which means two preliminary rounds, semifinal, and final. As long as we lose in the semifinal we're all right, and meanwhile we'll pick up loot in rounds one and two."

"As long as we do lose that semifinal . . ."

"Two of us out of four could make sure of that. I was going to tell you, anyway."

"And Bos and Lundiga?"

"What do you think?"

"You've *got* to tell them! Four out of four is more than twice as good as two when it comes to throwing a game."

"I guess you're right." Brad raised his voice: "Bos—Lundiga." In Latin, he said: "Now listen carefully . . ."

For these games even the upper classes arrived on time, and they followed the mob in making the Romans their favourites. Bos and Lundiga especially were cheered for almost every stroke. They won the first game easily and picked up a useful harvest of silver and gold.

Watching the next game in the tournament, Brad said: "The rackets really make a difference. Do you know, I think we could make it all the way through."

"Don't even think about it," Simon said.

Brad grinned. "Don't worry. I won't."

As the players came out for the game after that, Simon, who was looking at a girl in the front row with an intriguing face shadowed by an ornate headdress, heard Brad give a small whistle of surprise. What he saw as he looked down at the court was riveting. The players in one of the teams were carrying rackets very much like theirs.

Brad said: "Amazing how fast new ideas can get around."

"How do you think they found out how to make them?" Simon asked.

"From people who saw us at the washing place. By the next games, everyone will have them."

The team with rackets triumphed even more easily than they had, completely outplaying their opponents. They themselves won by six rings to three in the second round, without coming under pressure.

"That's it," Simon said, as they trooped off after collecting their booty. "The next we lose."

Throwing the game would have been easier, he felt, if they had been playing the team who had rackets, but they were in the other half of the draw. Their opponents this time were a team who, like the Gorillas, were strong on physical action; they had done a lot of damage to opponents in earlier rounds, breaking a leg of one of them. They started the same way against the Romans, and as Simon hit a wall and slid dazed to the ground he was thankful this was the last game and there was no need to make an effort. Brad was felled almost immediately afterwards. Then three converged on Bos, whose own reputation for toughness was well known. He, too, went down under the impact, though Lundiga, piling in on top, knocked one of his assailants off his feet at the same time.

What followed was staggering. There were some confused moments of struggle on the ground; then Bos rose up from the melee, scattering bodies around him. As they tried to get up, he smashed them back to the ground one after another, and with an amazing turn of speed chased the fourth and flattened him too. Lundiga was a dancing demon in his wake; she charged into one who was making a second attempt to rise and his head hit the wall with a sickening thump. As that happened Bos, in fury, scooped up the ball and drove it through the ring. It went round three walls before Lundiga picked it up and scored again, and, intercepting her own shot as it cannoned off the side wall, slammed it back through for a third. The pair of them seemed demented. Bos was going after the ball to make it four when Brad and Simon together grabbed his arm.

Simon howled: "You idiot! This is the one we lose. We've got to!"

Bos rubbed his head. He had a dazed expression.

"I forgot."

Their opponents were struggling to their feet. Brad said: "Don't forget again. They have to win."

It wasn't that easy. Bos had knocked the stuffing out of them, and they were slow to recover. Even when they were allowed to make their shots unchallenged, they couldn't score. The crowd, realizing the game had gone sour, started to hurl abuse at both sides. It seemed an age before the Aztecs finally got a ring, and after they had scored their second, time crawled again. Simon began deliberately offering them chances. It made the spectators still more furious, but he didn't care. When their opponents got their third ring, he waved his racket joyfully over his head. One more and they were safe, but even if the game ended right now there would be a play-off, and Bos and Lundiga could scarcely go crazy twice.

The ball came to him, and in high spirits he slammed it, aimlessly but well away from the ring. It hit a projecting piece of wood at the edge of the judges' box, came off at a crazy angle, and spun lazily through the air. In horror Simon shouted "No!" but that did nothing to stop it. Cleanly, not touching the sides, the ball dropped through the ring, and a moment later the judge dropped his scarf.

In the final, as they had expected would happen, they met the other team with rackets, who quickly proved even better on court than they had looked from the benches. They got a ring in the first minute, and soon after came close to getting a second. The crowd, soured by the way the Romans had played in the semifinal, were backing them strongly. Simon's legs were swept from under him while he was making a shot, and their howl of glee had a chilling sound. He was dazed by the fall, but images of priests wielding knives quickly brought him to his feet. He saw an Aztec shot bounce off the underside of the ring, and Lundiga collected the ball. She was not in a good position herself but got it across to Bos, and he slammed it home.

That slightly calmed his fears, but the respite did not last long: within five minutes, the Aztecs had scored their second. The game had become fast and furious, and the crowd's excitement was mounting. Trying to lose had been difficult, but needing to win as the alternative to a painful death was agony: the more effort he put in, the more ineffectual he felt.

Against the run of play, Lundiga tied the score, only to have the opposing captain pick up the ball from the service, sidewall it and run expertly into place to put his side ahead for the third time. The Aztecs continued to put pressure on, getting in at least three shots to one of theirs, and it was totally against expectation that a clever bit of combination play between Bos and Lundiga resulted in her tying the score for the third time.

A long period followed in which neither side scored. The more elusive the ring proved, the rougher the going got. It began to look as though this game really might be heading for a play-off, and Simon felt in no shape to face it. He was smashed to the ground for the twentieth time—or was it the hundredth?—and lay there, telling himself that getting back on his feet was not as impossible as it seemed. The screech of the spectators was a howl for blood. Painfully, he pulled himself up against a wall, and as he did saw Brad sandwiched by two of the Aztecs. He slumped, unconscious, and didn't look like rising again.

Simon himself could barely hobble. The Aztecs were getting in unchallenged shots, two of which hit the edge of the ring. Then Bos charged one of them as he was shooting, and as the ball went clear, Lundiga raced for it and hit it a swipe on the run. It struck the inside of the ring, and angled through.

Unexpected though it was, that had to be a winning shot. Up in their box, one of the judges was peering at the twine: the slow fuse must be approaching the end knot. Any instant the scarf must drop.

But it didn't, and the Aztecs swung back into attack. Brad lay where he had dropped, motionless. Lundiga and Bos were the only effective players left on their side, and they could not possibly cover all four Aztecs. Simon stared helplessly as one of them collared the ball and lobbed it gently to another standing unguarded and perfectly placed to shoot.

The Aztec had all the time in the world to take aim, and as he hit the ball Simon could tell it was dead on target. Then, it seemed out of nowhere, Lundiga catapulted herself up and sideways in a gigantic leap. With her arm fully stretched the tip of her racket made only glancing contact with the ball, but it was enough to deflect it from centre to edge. As it bounced back into the court, the scarf dropped.

While the defeated players trudged like zombies from the court, the crowd stamped and cheered, and those in the lower rows signalled approbation with a shower of largesse: Simon was hit quite painfully below the right eye by a jewelled brooch. The floor of the court turned silvery with, he was pleased to see, a nice sprinkling of feathery gold.

This did not by any means represent the whole of their winnings: a special prize of gold chains was awarded by the priesthood. The Chief Priest came on court for the presentation, attended by a gaggle of junior priests and a military escort. The lesser priests wore headdresses a couple of feet high, but his was twice that, a delicately balanced superstructure in which vermilion feathers sprouted from chunks of jade. His face was old and thin, his eyes weak and blinking. Wisps of white hair were visible through the red and green.

They had managed to revive Brad partially, but he was still in a daze. He wobbled as a chain was hung round his neck, and Simon put a hand on his arm to steady him. He realized that the unsteadiness was not entirely caused by exhaustion when a similar chain was dropped onto him; he looked at the soft yellow gleam on his chest and felt the massiveness of it weighing him down.

The procession passed to Bos, and finally to Lundiga. The Chief Priest had jabbered in Aztec at all of them, congratulations, presumably, or some kind of blessing, and hadn't seemed to bother about the lack of response. But his voice now took on a sharper, commanding note, and Simon was surprised to hear Lundiga say, in Latin: "It is not proper."

He came out of a gold-tinged reverie and looked at her. The Chief Priest's finger was pointing at her fur hat, and his tone of voice conveyed the message. He wanted the hat removed, and Lundiga was refusing.

The small weak eyes beneath the headdress stared into her face, and her blue eyes stared right back. The Chief Priest stepped back a pace, as though giving way. But then his brittle voice rapped out, and the captain of the guard jumped forward. Before Lundiga could realize what was happening, he had pulled the hat off her head.

There was a cry of wonder from the crowd, and gasps from those nearby. Lundiga's hair fell loose in a bright yellow cloud. Even with her figure shapeless under the playing jacket, no one could be in doubt of her being a girl.

For moments the Chief Priest went on staring; then he spoke again. His words were meaningless to Simon, but Brad shouted "No!" Soldiers moved to isolate Lundiga; she protested loudly, but they seized her arms. Bos, with a bull-like roar, threw himself at them, and Brad and Simon followed suit.

Simon's awareness of the futility of this was short-lived. Almost at once something smacked him on the back of the head, and he went out.

7

SIMON FIRST REALIZED that the face looking solicitously down into his was that of a pretty girl; second that he was lying on soft cushions. He had a moment of wondering if he were dead, and the Moslems had been right about the afterlife: instead of golden harps on clouds, timeless houris serving lemonade from a cup that never emptied. On the other hand his head was aching savagely, which didn't square with Paradise. He pulled himself up on an elbow, wincing, and saw Bos and Brad on couches similar to his own.

Bos said: "Are you well, Simonus?"

He closed his eyes and opened them again. "That's more than I'd like to say. Where are we?" Something of the events prior to his being knocked out came back, and he sat up properly. "Where's Lundiga?"

Bos gloomily shook his head. "We do not know."

Simon tried to think. "We attacked the guards. Why didn't they kill us? Why aren't we in a cell, at least?"

The couches were made of elaborate inlaid woods, the floor was covered with colourful rugs, and there were embroidered hangings on the walls with quite a bit of gold thread in the embroidery. In niches on the walls were jade carvings, some of them fairly large. Three girls were in attendance. The one who had wakened him proffered a cup—polished wood with a silver rim. He was thirsty and drank; it wasn't lemonade but a very pleasant fruit drink.

Brad said: "What do you mean, a cell? We're the champs, kings of the heap." His voice was flat. "We're booked in at the Palzibil Hilton, on an unlimited expense account."

Simon said: "I don't get it. What about Lundiga?"

"The winners of the games can get away with just about everything, I guess, including assaulting the military. Soldiers aren't sacred, you see, even when they're attending the Chief Priest. If one of us had laid a finger on him, it would have been different. Very different, I should think."

Simon's recollections were hazy. He remembered the weight of the gold chain . . . Lundiga saying "It is not proper" . . . her hair cascading . . .

"Just what did happen? The Chief Priest wanted Lundiga's hat off. Was it because she'd disobeyed him that he told the guards to grab her?"

"No."

Simon said: "Because he discovered she was a girl, then? There's a rule against girls taking part in the games?"

"There may be; I don't know. But it wasn't that. It was her hair."

"Her hair? I suppose it seemed a bit striking, since the Aztecs are all brunettes. But I don't see . . ."

"Not just striking," Brad said. "The word is unique. The only blonde they've ever seen. That made her something extremely special. Too special for ordinary mortals, according to the Chief Priest. He claimed her as a bride for the gods."

"What does that mean?"

Brad was not looking at him but the ceiling. "Those young girls they sacrifice at the top of the pyramid—they're called brides of the gods."

If his mind hadn't been so fuzzy, Simon thought, he would have known something like that was involved: there was nothing amiable about the Aztec religion. He felt a wave of revulsion and anger, and said: "We've got to do something."

Brad looked at him. "What?"

He got rockily to his feet. "I don't know. But something anyway—not just lie here, being waited on."

"Look out the window." Brad's voice had a weary impatience. "This room is about forty feet above street level. There are four armed guards outside in the corridor, and another forty within call. If you want to fight your way out go ahead, and the best of British luck."

Simon glanced at Bos, who shrugged helplessly. The gesture was a total confirmation of Brad's words, especially since it was Lundiga who was at risk. He had not shared Brad's and Simon's reservations about her; to him she was simply a marvellous girl, a substitute for the daughter which a gladiator's life had denied him.

Simon said: "They won't have done anything to her yet?"

"No."

"Can you be sure?"

Brad said: "I've picked up a few things from eavesdropping on the guards. They're not keeping her in Palzibil, first of all. She's being taken to the capital, Tenochtitlan, where the chief temple is. The only blonde in the Aztec empire is too important for a local show."

Brad's matter-of-factness annoyed Simon. He said: "So what happens now?"

"As far as we're concerned, nothing much. The Chief Priest may have requisitioned Lundiga for the gods, but the rest of us are heroes. We won the ball game, didn't we? We were taken into custody when we fought with the guards, but it's no more than a kind of house arrest. They'll let us loose in a few days, providing we give them no further trouble."

"After which we can live a life of ease on what we picked up from the games?"

"That's right."

"Providing we give no trouble?"

Brad nodded.

"While Lundiga's carted off to be sacrificed to their gods?"

Brad shrugged.

Simon turned angrily to Bos: "What do *you* think of that for an idea?"

Brad spoke: "The trouble with you is not simply being dumb, but assuming other people are. Ritual sacrifices take place at the major religious ceremonies. What I've also found out is that the next is fixed for the next full moon but one. Till then Lundiga's safe, and that gives us time to do something about rescuing her. But before we can start making any sort of plan, we ourselves need to be free, which we probably will be in a matter of days, providing we're good little boys meanwhile. Is anything getting through that thick skull of yours?"

Bos said: "Bradus is right, Simonus. There is an old Roman proverb: hasten slowly."

Simon felt his head starting to ache again. "Yes," he said. "I've heard it."

On the fourth morning of their incarceration, the guard commander indicated that they should follow him. Outside, a palanquin capable of carrying four in comfort was waiting with its attendant bearers, six to each pole. It was lined with gaudy cloths and feathers and a lot of gold leaf. It was the governor's private vehicle, in fact, and, supported on the shoulders of the trotting slaves, it conveyed them to the governor's palace.

There they were made much of, and lavishly fed. They were also given bags of silver and gold: yet another bonus from their victory. The Aztecs' passion for the games extended to heavy gambling on the outcome, and the champions picked up a percentage of the winning bets.

There were three lots of bags; no reference was made to a fourth, or to Lundiga. Presumably her share went to the priests. Simon had argued with Brad that they should make some complaint, or at least inquiry, about Lundiga—that not to do so might rouse suspicion. Brad had disagreed. The Aztecs would see nothing odd in their displaying indifference to her fate. Their own fear of the gods and the priesthood was such that they would be prepared to hand over their closest kin without protest at a priest's behest. Nodding and smiling in response to the flattery of the Aztec nobles, Simon was forced to conclude Brad had been right. In the games Lundiga had been given the greatest applause, but as far as they were concerned now, she had never existed.

He had had no favourable view of the rich Aztecs, and he decided he liked them even less on close contact. He forced himself to endure the socializing, thankful that, as foreigners, they weren't expected to do more than nod and smile, and was relieved when the governor's withdrawal signalled the party's end.

The good bit was that this marked the termination of their detention: the guard commander returned with them, but only to collect his troops. Watching the soldiers march away, Brad said: "Right. We can start making plans."

"This place where they've taken Lundiga," Simon asked, "—what did you say it was called?"

"Tenochtitlan."

"And where is it?"

"After Cortes and his conquistadores destroyed it—in our world—Mexico City was built on the ruins."

"So how far away?"

"Well, if I'm right in thinking Palzibil is located somewhere near Sumter, South Carolina, more than two thousand miles, as the llama trots."

"More than two thousand miles! But that would take months. And the ceremony's less than two months away."

Brad was unperturbed. "These highways are pretty good. I think you could go as much as seventy miles a day, with fast llamas. Four or five weeks, even so. But there's another way, apart from Incan roads, in which this Aztec empire is different from the one the Spaniards conquered. Those Aztecs weren't seagoing—I don't think they had anything bigger than inshore fishing skiffs. But I've learned from Strong Feather that these Aztecs have boats that cross the Gulf of Mexico. It's a natural development with an empire that stretches both north and south of it. That will cut the distance by nearly a third, and the time by a lot more."

"When do we start?"

"Easy. Remember that Roman proverb. We have things to do first."

"What things?" Simon asked.

"Finding out more details about the route, first off. And then getting hold of llamas—racing llamas if there are such things."

"Won't that seem a bit odd?"

"Why should it? We're filthy rich, remember. It's no different from a Wimbledon champion buying himself a Ferrari."

Among other things, their new status in society entitled them to wear headdresses; in fact, representatives of the headdress makers' guild insisted on providing them with exotic specimens of their art. Viewing himself in a polished bronze mirror, Bos protested that he would not wear anything so ludicrous.

"You have to, Bos," Brad said. "All the big ball players do."

"I look like a woman!"

"Not really." He managed not to smile. "And remember, it's in a good cause."

They bought llamas at a farm west of the city which was said to have the best in the province: the Aztec breeder was proud to demonstrate the speed and general quality of his beasts. Since they were ignorant foreigners, he offered riding instruction, and was impressed by their quickness in learning, unaware of their previous horse-riding experience or, for that matter, of the existence of such a thing as a horse. The swaying camel-like motion was different, but they adapted to it.

The following afternoon, Brad said: "I reckon we're ready to go. I've been picking Strong Feather's brains again.

There's a port called Xicocoaz about four hundred miles south, from which ships cross to the western shore of the Gulf. I figure if we really push these llamas along, we can make it in five days. We should be able to keep comfortably ahead of anyone who decided to come after us, but having a head start would help. If we leave at dawn tomorrow . . ."

"What about the servants?" Simon asked.

The three girls had remained with them, and they had also acquired a household staff of another twenty or so.

"I thought of that. They'll expect us, as foreigners, to have our own religion. We'll tell them there's a holy day coming up, and we have to spend twenty-four hours in solitary prayer. It's a reason for sending them away this evening."

"Do you think they'll buy it?"

"They have to," Brad said. "They're servants and we're masters. But being religious nuts, they won't even find it strange."

Bos touched his headdress. "We can leave these behind?"

"I'm afraid not. They're worn on journeys, as you've seen. If we're on llamas we belong to the upper crust, and members of the upper crust wear headdresses. And there's something else you're not going to like, Bos."

Bos looked at him suspiciously: "What?"

"That beard of yours has got to come off."

"No! I will wear this comic thing, if you say I must, but I will not shave off my beard."

"We can't afford to attract attention. For Lundiga, Bos."

The big man groaned, but did not argue further.

Unlike Roman cities, where there was considerable nocturnal activity with rumbling carts and roistering merry-makers often until dawn, Aztec cities were silent and unpeopled after dark; even the homeless did not stir from their patches. The llamas were tethered in the house's ground-floor colonnade. Their saddlebags held rations for the journey, and also gold and silver; Simon heard it chink as they rode through the deserted streets.

Dawn was just lighting the sky. Stone buildings gave way to hovels and then to open country: they heard the gobble of turkeys, and pigs grunting. The climate had continued to improve as the region's short winter retreated, and it was not cold. The sun rose behind the green screen of an avocado grove, its rays splintering into shards that dazzled the eye.

Soon cultivated land gave way in turn to scrub and woodland. The road remained empty; except at certain special times, usually connected with religious festivals, journeying between cities was not common. It was amazing, Simon thought, that so much effort had been put into building highways that were so little used, though the superabundance of labour did make the extravagance more understandable. And, at least, unlike motorways crumbling beneath the weight of juggernaut lorries, these would probably last a thousand years without maintenance.

They had their first encounter some hours after leaving the city: with a llama-rider heading the opposite way. A purple band on his sleeve proclaimed him as imperial messenger, and official-looking satchels hung from his saddle. He saluted them respectfully but did not speak. Bos turned his head to watch him. "He will speak of seeing us."

"He'll mention seeing three riders," Brad said. "There'll be no reason to connect it with us till the servants report us missing. Even if they come after us, it's going to be too late to make a start today. And we've got the fastest beasts available."

At dusk they found a watering place for the llamas, and tethered them for the night. Trying to get comfortable on a patch of moss, Simon decided it didn't take long to be spoilt for life in the open. It would have been nice to lie on cushions, with his serving wench bringing him chocolate. But the day's riding, which had left him with aching muscles, had also tired him. He did not stay awake long and slept soundly.

There was an intervening city which they passed through by moonlight, seeing no one. In late afternoon of the fifth day they looked down from high ground to a dazzle of water. Within an hour they had reached Xicocoaz, and rode through busy streets to the harbour. The boats bobbing at the wharves were not impressive compared with the *Stella*, or even with a Viking longship: they had a very shallow draft and seemed to have been made of skins, sewn and caulked over a bamboo framework.

They were lucky in finding a boat almost ready to cast off. It was already full, in fact, in Simon's view overloaded; but the captain was prepared to make room for three extra at a price. Negotiations on that point did not take long. Bos pointed to the llamas, and indicated that they were offering them as a straight swap for their passage.

The expression on the captain's face made it clear this was well over the odds for three tickets to ride, and he ushered them on board with a great show of deference, ordering other passengers in the stern to make a place for them. Simon was not too happy about this, since those moved included a frail-looking woman and an old man, but knew they must comply with Aztec custom. And Aztec custom, where this sort of thing was concerned, was strict and simple: the rich got all the privileges, and the poor got all the kicks.

The voyage lasted five days, and long before it was over they were glad of the extra space: most passengers had barely room enough to lie down. They were fortunate in having calm seas and a favourable wind; they learned a week was the more usual duration for a trip, and two weeks not uncommon. Cooking was going on all day long. A wood-fired oven was in operation, dangerously close to the mast and flapping sail, and the crew operated a rota against payment in cocoa beans. Nothing was demanded from the Romans though, and Simon suspected that if their rations had run out, others would have been made to feed them.

The boat entered harbour in the early morning. The port itself was unimpressive: wooden jetties extended from low stone wharves. Beyond, there was a handful of stone buildings surrounded by the usual shacks. But it was a relief to stand on a surface that did not roll under you.

Bos said: "When we have found Lundiga, where do we go, Bradus—to this country of yours in the west?"

"I think so."

"Can we get there by land?"

"Yes."

"That is good. Because if there were more sea voyaging, I think you would have to go without me. Our Christian symbol is the fish, but I will be happy to die without seeing the sea again."

If the entry port had been unimpressive, Tenochtitlan more than made up for it. It was many times the size of the cities they had seen so far; in fact, it was more like a complex of cities. It had been built on four separate but linked lakes, and everywhere white buildings towered over lagoons and canals; there was as great a traffic by boat as there was by road. Close by the causeway along which they entered ran a gigantic aqueduct of masonry, as imposing as any in the Roman empire.

The city's centre stood on an island surrounded by a considerable breadth of water on which small pleasure boats and big barges plied. The barges were mostly mercantile, but one with a great yellow-and-red awning obviously belonged to someone of importance. The causeway continued on through a quarter of increasingly prosperous-looking houses to a great battlemented square in which there were fountains and palaces. There was also the pyramid, which was the temple of the gods. It was at least twice the height of the one in Palzibil. At intervals all round it statues of the gods squatted on blocks of dull blackish stone, glowering down at the spectator. They represented many different deities, but had one thing in common: a look of cruel contempt for their worshippers.

The city and suburbs were full of bustle and activity. Its markets and arcades sold every imaginable commodity and some which Simon could never have guessed: one entire quarter was reserved for stalls selling the feathers of eagles and other birds of prey. The population was polyglot, with Indians from South America as well as North.

The size and complexity of the place at least made it easier not to attract attention; even if word of their disappearance should come from Palzibil they were unlikely to be discovered in this teeming stew of humanity. West of the central square was an area occupied by the rich, many acres in extent. They rented one of the more modest houses there, together with a household staff of slaves. It was furnished with frescoes and painted carvings Simon could have done without. Several depicted gory battle scenes, and there were graphic illustrations of human sacrifice. A particularly unwelcome one showed the aftermath of a battle, with prisoners being tortured in various unpleasant ways. It was all too vivid a reminder of the possibilities arising from an unsuccessful outcome to the enterprise.

Their most urgent need was for information about Lundiga, and for that they did not have long to wait. As in all capital cities gossip was rife, and the maiden with hair like threads of gold provided a main topic of conversation. Some stories had it that her hair truly was of that metal, and an embellishment provided her with fingernails and toenails of jade. There were varying accounts of her origin. Some made her a visitor from lands beyond the sunset, while others ventured into the realms of the entirely fanciful: she had arrived riding a llama with a golden hide . . . she had come out of the sea at sunrise . . . she had flown into Tenochtitlan on the back of a giant eagle . . .

But if there was no consistency here, there was unanimity as to her present whereabouts. Everyone knew she was in the care of the Arch-Priest, in his palace at the summit of the pyramid of the gods.

They went back to take a more considered look at it. The experience was disheartening. Apart from being so much higher than the one in Palzibil, it occupied a far greater area: the four base lines were about half a mile in length. And near the top the steep inward pitch of the walls reversed itself, creating an overhang under a long blank parapet. Access to the top was by ramps on the northern and southern sides. Each was guarded by armed men, and they established that this was a twenty-four hour guard. The men on duty were replaced by fresh detachments at dawn and dusk.

While a tropical storm deluged the city with warm rain, they discussed possibilities. Simon said: "We can rule out direct assault. Short of inventing the cannon there's no way of getting past those guards, and we haven't time enough for that."

"I do not know what this cannon thing is," Bos said, "but I have known Roman soldiers who could be bribed. And we have money."

"More than twenty men," Simon said, "plus the guard commander. And all answerable to the Arch-Priest, who's got a very well-equipped torture chamber. And anyway, could we trust them? They could take the money and turn us in. It's not just a question of getting in there, but of getting Lundiga out. I don't think any money could buy the golden girl."

"No," Brad said. "That wouldn't work."

"So what's left?" Simon asked. "Start a revolution and overthrow this empire, too? We don't have a lot of time for that, either."

"And we don't speak the language well enough. And there's no group like the Christians ready to rebel. We can forget revolutions."

Silence followed, broken only by the slash of rain and the distant gurgle of water in the gutters. The prospects were not just bleak, but hopeless. No amount of derring-do on their part was going to help Lundiga; there was no way of rescuing her.

They would have done better, Simon thought, to stay in Palzibil than to come to the city where the horror was to take place. In fact it was unthinkable that they should be here on the day of the sacrifice, listening to the bloodthirsty howls of the mob. He was wondering how to voice that without seeming callous and indifferent to Lundiga's fate, when Brad put a question. "Can you climb?"

Bos asked: "Climb what?"

Simon said: "The pyramid, do you mean? It would be pretty difficult anyway, but that overhang at the top makes it impossible."

Brad said: "I did some rock-climbing the summer before—" he glanced at Bos—"before you and I were shipwrecked and washed up on the shore of Britain. You can get past overhangs with pitons. It wouldn't be easy with solid rock, but there are crevices between the blocks one could hammer into. I think it might go."

Simon visualized himself upside-down beneath the overhang, with a three-hundred-feet drop below. He said: "Where do we get pitons for a starter?"

"Bronze chisels. That's something else the Aztecs got from conquering the Incas: a lesson in metallurgy. Stone chisels and a stone hammer would have made it a lot more difficult."

"Are you serious?"

Brad paid no attention. "I've done some climbing, as I say. And I'm the lightest. If I can get past that overhang, then winch you two up . . ."

Simon said: "It won't . . ."

He was overridden by Bos. "I do not understand all you say, but if you think it possible, Bradus, we will do it."

"But . . ."

"It is that or leaving Lundiga to the priest's knife."

Bos looked at Simon, not reproachfully but like a man explaining things to a child or someone mentally deficient.

"We must try."

8

THE MOON WAS A THIN CRESCENT of silver against starlight—the storm had passed over and the night was warm and windless—as they slipped through the shadows. They wore belted jackets and rope sandals, and Bos had the coil of rope hooked over one shoulder. The bag with the hammer and bronze pegs hung from Brad's belt. Simon was unencumbered, and glad of it.

The sight of the wall they proposed climbing made him feel terrible. It towered vastly over them, gleaming dimly in the faint light, seeming almost sheer. It was too dark to see the top, which was just as well; merely imagining it, and what Brad was proposing to do, made him queasy. Brad paid out a length of rope on which they were to secure themselves. He tied it as he had been shown. Brad whispered: "OK. I'm going, Simon. Follow when the rope tautens."

He set off, hauling himself up the wall, and all too soon Simon felt a tug on the rope. He closed his mind to everything except reaching high, hooking fingertips over the ledge above, heaving himself up, finding a foothold, reaching out again. . .

Brad's voice whispered overhead.

"OK. Twitch for Bos to start."

They climbed steadily, occasionally pausing to rest. That meant standing with one's face pressed against stone and leaning inwards: the ledges between the blocks were just wide enough to accommodate the ball of a foot. It wasn't bad once you settled into a rhythm. They seemed to have come a long way, but Simon didn't feel like looking down to check. Nor up; it was better to keep his eyes fixed on the wall.

Resting, with Brad climbing, he indulged in a daydream in which this was over and they were on their way again. He excluded thought of Lundiga: there seemed no point. He imagined the hazards they might encounter: hostile natives, hunger and thirst, poisonous snakes . . . At least it would all take place on level ground.

The sky exploded, and automatically he looked up. The sound was like the rattle of dozens, hundreds of machine guns, and he pressed himself in against the wall to escape the hail of bullets. The rattling continued, louder and spreading wider. Moon and stars were obliterated by a cloud that flowed out, and he wondered, stupidly, if the pyramid itself was collapsing—if their climb had disturbed some delicate equilibrium and it was falling apart. Then the cloud started thinning and breaking into individual particles, and he could see they were birds, flapping away into the night.

His heart was thumping and he had to take several deep breaths. Brad had disturbed a roosting site. There must have been thousands of them. Unnerving as it had been for him, it must have been much worse for Brad. He whispered up: "Are you all right?"

There was a pause. "Sure."

"I thought . . ."

"No talking. Those guards . . ."

He did not need to finish: the bird flight could have aroused curiosity. Without thinking, Simon looked down. He saw no movement, but the realization of how high they had come frightened the life out of him, and he quickly looked away.

At last he heard the slight noise of Brad resuming the climb, and followed in his turn. Another hazard for which the birds were responsible emerged when he found his fingers not gripping bare stone but digging into a layer of slimy droppings. It was not only nauseating, but made climbing a lot more difficult. He hoped it might mean they were nearing the top, but after some minutes the wall was clean, and Brad was still going up.

He began to tire, and he had to halt and massage a cramp out of his right leg. The realization that he was holding things up caused him to set off again before the pain had completely eased, and it continued to hurt. It was once more starting to get unbearable, when Brad whispered: "I've reached it. Come on up."

Simon did some further massage on his leg while Bos climbed to his level; then they went up the rest of the way together. Brad had driven a peg into one of the grooves between the slabs of stone, and he now tested its firmness by tugging at it.

Simon said: "Want any help?"

Brad was fitting in another peg. "No, I'll do it. It's

supposed to take my weight if I fall, and I'll feel happier if I've done it myself."

The hammering seemed loud, but they were so far above the ground it probably didn't matter. Just over their heads the overhang blotted out the sky. He tried to estimate the length of it: ten feet, maybe twelve. Too long for comfort.

"Right," Brad said. "Here I go. Anchor yourselves to these pegs when I move on. It may help, if I crash."

"Anything else we can do?" Simon asked.

"Not a lot. A prayer would do no harm."

"I have been praying all the way," Bos said. "But I will pray harder."

Brad drove a peg in higher. He had loops of rope on either side of his belt, and once the peg was firm he hooked one over it. He swung free, hanging from the peg, and Simon braced himself against the wall. He could hear Brad's laboured breathing, and the sound of another peg going in.

The process was maddeningly slow, and having to listen to Bos muttering Latin didn't help. After some time he heard an exclamation, and something just missed his head. A peg struck the step beneath them, and clattered down the side of the pyramid. It seemed a long time before the noise died away. He thought of the guards and wondered if Brad would suspend operations, but the hammering restarted immediately. He was right, of course: the only thing that mattered now was getting past the overhang.

At last, craning his head back, Simon could see Brad's outline against the sky. He had his hands on the parapet and was trying to heave himself up. Something was holding him back. He contorted his body desperately, and Simon realized his rope was caught on the peg below. If Brad were to fall now . . . He braced himself harder. Bos had abandoned prayer and was urging Brad: "You can do it, lad!"

There was a wrenching sound of the peg coming out; it too whistled past Simon's ear. Brad twisted and heaved again; at first ineffectually but then he disappeared over the top. His voice came down: "I'll make the rope secure. Hang on."

There was a long interval before he spoke again: "I think it's OK. You first, Simon. You're lighter."

Hesitation was not going to improve things. He gave a sharp testing tug on the rope and started climbing, his feet treading the wall. It was not all that difficult, providing he could keep his mind closed to the drop. That wasn't easy, though.

Pain shot through his right hand and he gave an involuntary yelp of pain: his fingers had been trapped between rope and stone. But that meant he was nearly there; he looked up to see the parapet's edge clear-cut against the sky. He reached for it, found a grip, and heaved convulsively. Brad helped him over the top and he collapsed thankfully on the other side.

As he got up he said to Brad: "What did you use to anchor the rope?"

"There wasn't anything. I just dug in my toes against the bottom of the parapet."

He was glad he hadn't known that earlier. At least there were two of them to haul up Bos, though even so it was a strain. Once he had joined them, Simon could take stock of the situation.

All it was possible to make out in the dim light was that the top was level and had quite a number of buildings on it. The parapet stretched out of view in either direction. It must enclose a considerable area: enough to house a small village. Brad said: "Any suggestions what we do next?"

It was an unusual query to come from him. His voice had a note of exhaustion. It was obvious the climb had taken a lot out of him. Simon was conscious of a similar reaction, of feeling at a loss about what to do next. Bos, though, said, matter-of-factly: "She is somewhere up here. We must look till we find her."

The first building they tackled had an open door, and it wasn't difficult to establish that it contained what a sound of snoring had already suggested—a score or so of sleeping men. The second proved identical. After a row of these huts, they came on smaller ones. The first was an ablutions room, with stone basins on either side and a pool in the centre.

Subsequently they found storerooms, a kitchen, and next to it, a messroom. Simon began to get discouraged again, and it even occurred to him to wonder if the information about her being here had been correct; supposing she were, the chances of finding her without their being discovered first did not seem high. Then Bos gripped his arm, whispering "Look."

He peered into the darkness and saw a building much bigger than any they had so far encountered, higher as well as broader. Bos led the investigation, and they found a doorway with a bead curtain that jangled slightly as they pushed through. They passed from the room inside to a second and a third; they seemed to be well furnished. But empty. Simon whispered to Brad: "Nothing here. Shall we move on?"

"Over there," Brad whispered back, "—isn't it a staircase?"

The stairs creaked alarmingly under their feet. There was a landing at the top, and rooms on either side. To the left there was a sound of rhythmic breathing; Simon and Bos peeped in and saw about a dozen pallet beds. At that point Simon became aware Brad was not with them, and turned to see him beckoning from the entrance to the room opposite.

This room had just one bed and one sleeping figure. It would be marvellous if it were Lundiga, Simon thought; except it couldn't possibly be. Then the figure moved, flinging out an arm and turning over in bed. Blonde hair gleamed in the faint moonlight.

Leaning over her, Bos whispered urgently: "Lundiga . . . wake up, girl!"

She shifted but did not respond; she had always been a heavy sleeper. Bos shook the outstretched arm. "Wake up. It's us."

She sat up abruptly, grabbing at his wrist. "What . . . who?" She came wide-awake. "Is it you, Bos?" She was incredulous. "And Simonus? And Bradus!"

Brad said: "Quiet, Lundiga. You'll wake them."

She paid no attention. "How did you get here? Were you brought?" The tone of incredulity deepened. "In the middle of the night?"

"We climbed the pyramid," Brad said.

"Climbed? Why?"

"Not so loud," Brad pleaded. "The thing is, we can get you out of here. But for Odin's sake, whisper."

As Lundiga started to speak again, in a voice only slightly lower, Simon heard a patter of feet. He swung round, but they were already on him, and he was borne down by clutching arms. Soft flesh pressed against his face. There was a general babble in which he distinguished Bos's voice raised in anger, and Lundiga's also raised but speaking Aztec. He had just worked out that the bodies holding him down were female when the pressure relaxed and he was able to get up from the floor. There were girls everywhere. Lundiga spoke again, and they scurried from the room. Turning to them, she said: "I have sent for lamps. And food and drink. You will need refreshment if you have climbed the pyramid!"

They looked at her. Brad shook his head.

"I don't understand the setup, but you've got rid of them. Now let's get out while we have the chance."

"Get out? Why?"

He said in exasperation: "Because you're in danger here. We all are. You must know that."

Lundiga shook her head emphatically. "I am in no danger. Nor are you. There was no need for your climbing—you only had to speak to the guards. I was expecting you to come. I sent messengers to Palzibil to fetch you."

Bos spoke patiently. "I do not know what lies they have told you, Lundiga, but you must not believe them. They plan to sacrifice you to their cruel gods."

"Sacrifice me?" She laughed. "I do not think so!"

Brad said: "Listen. I heard what the Chief Priest at Palzibil said when he ordered his guards to take you. He claimed you as a bride of the god. And that's exactly what they call the girls who are sacrificed: brides of the gods. Look, we haven't time to argue. Just accept that I know what I'm talking about, and let's get going."

She smiled affectionately at him. "You know a great deal, Bradus. I have never known anyone who knew so much. But even you do not know everything. I have learned things since I was brought here. It is true the girls who are sacrificed are called brides of the gods. But those are the *lesser* gods. There is a greater god they worship, compared with whom even the God of War and the Rain God are nothing. He is called Ipalnemohuani, which means the One by Whom We Live. He is like your Christian god, because they say he made all things. They worship him, but they do not offer him sacrifices."

Brad said: "You seem to have learned the language pretty thoroughly to have picked all that up." He sounded disgruntled.

Lundiga shrugged.

"The priests talk with me, and at other times I talk with my serving girls. It passes the time. And I think it is good to know the language of the people who are to worship me."

"Worship you!"

"Yes. The brides of the other gods are sacrificed, because it is easy to find new ones. But no bride has ever been chosen for Ipalnemohuani. That is because legend says that his bride will have hair of gold. And that is why I have been chosen to be his bride, and to be worshipped along with him." She giggled. "I do not think it will be so bad, being a goddess!"

They were interrupted by the return of the serving girls, bringing food and drink on gold trays. They also brought lamps and set them up in niches along the walls. Simon was able to see that the furnishings were sumptuous, with a vast amount of gold leaf.

Bos drained his pot, and had it refilled. Wiping his mouth with the back of his hand, he said: "I do not know about this goddess matter. The true God has no wife, though He has a mother. But we know these are heathens, and at least they seem to be looking after you well. Though I think it a poor prospect if you must spend the rest of your days up here in the sky."

Lundiga shook her head. "I do not have to do that. I shall stay here only until they have built me a palace. There is to be a summer palace also, in the hills." She waved a careless hand. "And others, I think, in other parts of the empire."

"It sounds pretty good," Simon said, "but you won't really be a free agent, will you? In a way you'll be a prisoner."

Her smile had just a touch of condescension.

"A goddess is not a prisoner, Simonus. These girls are my servants but the priests also serve me. Even the Arch-Priest. Whatever I wish, I can have. When I asked for you three to be brought, messengers were at once sent to Palzibil."

"Terrific," Brad said drily.

"It is even better than you think." She favoured him with another fond look. "I am to be the bride of Ipalnemohuani, but the God Who Made All Things has no body. I have told the Arch-Priest I require a human consort, and in this too my wish is a command. That is why I sent the messengers to Palzibil. You will share my good fortune. I will have a palace built for you, Bos, and Simonus—a palace each, if you wish."

She cast another warm and possessive glance at Brad.

"But Bradus—Bradus will share my throne, and be my consort!"

Eventually Lundiga dismissed them. She needed sleep, she said, yawning, because there was to be a rehearsal of her part in the full moon ceremony later that day, and she needed to prepare herself. They retired to the room the servants had prepared for them. The mattresses were down filled. Bos dropped on his and grunted approval.

"So fortune smiles on us again. We have found Lundiga, safe and well. And she says she will give us palaces to live in. She is a good girl."

Dawn was breaking through the windows. Lying down, Simon realized how tired he was. Yawning himself, he said: "A palace for you, Bos, and one for me. But the big prize goes to Bradus. He gets to marry a goddess."

Brad said: "Shut up."

"And the really big question," Simon went on, "is: does that make you a god? I figure it should."

"I said shut up!"

The note of real anger got through the haze of weariness. Simon looked at Brad and saw how tight his face was. He said: "Don't get steamed up. It's just a joke."

"Not to her."

Simon thought about that. "Well, no, maybe not. But the wedding won't take place yet awhile. You're both a bit young. You'll have time to wriggle out of it."

"I'm *getting* out, now."

"Out of Tenochtitlan? Let's think about it; in a day or two."

Brad shook his head stubbornly. "Now. Right away."

"There's no sense in that."

"Isn't there? Right now she's asleep, and she's had no time to give instructions. She will when she wakes up. We're going to be guarded; certainly, I am. Those messengers she sent to Palzibil weren't to ask if we wanted to come here—they were to bring us."

"Come on," Simon said, "you're taking it too seriously. This is Lundiga we're talking about—the Lundiga who saved us on the island, who was with us all those months. She may have some funny notion about making you her consort, but she's not going to try forcing you into anything."

"It's also the future bride of Ipalnemohuani we're talking about. A goddess. You heard what she said: 'It is good to know the language of the people who are to worship me.' She's living the part already."

"That's just a phase. She's too level-headed."

"'Power tends to corrupt; absolute power corrupts absolutely.' One of your English lords said that, and I think he had something. You can't get more absolute than a goddess. Anyway, I'm not taking any chances."

"Even if you should be right, we can always find a means of getting away."

"Climb down the pyramid, you mean, like we climbed up? I'd rather walk out, while I can."

His arguments were logical but not, Simon thought, entirely rational. While he was racking his brain for something else to say, Bos said slowly: "You are serious in this, Bradus. Because of Lundiga, you are determined to run away?"

"Yes."

"The pouch with my vine roots is in that place where we were living."

"We can pick it up, and the rest of the gear as well. She'll sleep till noon. The rehearsal's not till this afternoon."

There was a pause, before Bos said: "It is time they were planted. The soil here is good, and the climate too." The look he gave Brad was almost pleading. "And I do not think you need me any longer, Bradus, do you?"

Simon saw a look of unhappiness cross Brad's face fleetingly, but he quickly grinned. "Of course I don't. I don't need either of you. 'He travels the fastest who travels alone,' as Kipling said."

Bos gave a troubled shake of the head. "I do not know of this man Kip Ling. But if you *did* need me . . ."

"No," Brad said. "Plant your vines, Bos. I'll be better off on my own. And in fact you can do me a favour by staying. You can tell Lundiga I'm heading south, and get her search parties pointed in the wrong direction."

Simon's mind swam with tiredness. The urge to lie down and sleep was almost overwhelming; the idea of setting out on the trail again, by contrast, one of the most unappealing he could recall. He said: "It only needs one for that. We're relying on you, Bos."

"You will go with Bradus?" The broad face with its grizzled stubble of beard showed relief.

Brad said: "No need. In fact, you're not wanted."

"Don't be silly," Simon said. "When she finds she can't have you, she'll realize how good-looking I am. I don't fancy being the husband of a goddess, either. Let's go."

"Now, look . . ."

"We're wasting time, and you can't stop me." He turned to Bos. "One other thing. When those vines of yours have grown and fruited, and you've pressed wine from the grapes, lift the first glass to us."

Bos smiled, nodding. "That I will, Simonus."

9

ALL DAY THEY HAD SLOGGED through barren country—bare rock and coarse sand with patches of arid scrub—under a savage sun. They had seen no living thing apart from lizards, hovering vultures, a rattlesnake poised and watchful. Thirst was constant and maddening; from time to time they moistened their lips from the gourds they carried. Only moistened: they did not know when they would next find a waterhole. A couple of times already they had come close to death from thirst, and third time might not be so lucky. Simon, when he pressed the gourd briefly against cracked lips, shook it before putting it back on his belt. Less than half full; a lot less.

They had learned not to talk on the march: silence conserved energy. Brad, as he had done all along, had the advance position, with Simon a yard or so behind. It was Brad who had plotted their course along the Gulf coast, northeast along the Rio Grande; then the break west through mountainous country in search of the westward-flowing Gila River.

Simon had been content to let him make the decisions, and make the running, too. It was his country; he who had a destination in view. And despite the difficulties and dangers, the plan had worked so far, even to the extent of their finding the Gila . . . or some other wide river that flowed into the sunset. It was Brad, too, who had provided the drive to keep them going. Simon was aware he owed his life to that. The first time they had run out of water, a few days after heading into the hills, he had been ready to lie down and die. Brad had kept him moving; in the end almost dragging him along.

When hazards did not threaten, boredom was the enemy: the tedium of putting one foot in front of another, of plodding on. It was possible, Simon had discovered, to disconnect a part of his mind from his surroundings—to be, even while sweating under the relentless sun, at ease in the cool shade of a Roman villa, chatting with Lavinia while big red fish swam in the pool at their feet. Or, further back still, to be in that world which had the same physical contours as this and yet was so different, watching a cricket match from the pavilion, padded up to go in, meanwhile eating a bowl of strawberries and cream . . .

The strawberries and cream were a mistake. His dry mouth tried to salivate and failed; and his mind, rejecting the daydream, shunted him back to present reality. They had come over a rise and the way ahead was downhill. His eye scanned the horizon automatically. It registered what it saw, and transmitted the information to his brain. But this, too, his mind rejected: it could not be true. And yet it was—

the distant gleam was no illusion. How could Brad have failed to see it?

He croaked: "Look . . ."

Brad halted and turned slowly, almost painfully, towards him.

"No," Simon said. "In front . . ."

Brad still did not look that way. "What?"

"It's the sea."

It took them the rest of the day to get there; as they looked at breakers crashing onto shingle, the sun's disk was half lost in the waves, casting a crimson path towards the shore. Simon found a ledge and sat down, while Brad stood staring at the ocean. From the moment they had glimpsed the sea, there had been a reversal in their roles, with Simon eagerly pressing forward, Brad dragging behind.

"We've made it," Simon said.

"Yes." Brad's voice was listless.

"I don't think I really believed we ever would."

Brad said nothing.

"And you saw there's a river, a couple of miles north? Fresh water. It might be worth doing some fishing. We might catch us a salmon. Or a sardine—I'm not fussy."

It wasn't much of a joke, but even if he didn't think it rated a smile, Simon felt Brad could have made some sort of acknowledgement, instead of just staring at the sea. He felt himself getting annoyed, but controlled it. Concentrate on what matters, he thought: we've done it, and it was no pushover.

He said: "This is a poor spot for bivouacking. There'll be more shelter by the river. I saw trees."

Brad still said nothing. Simon stood up and took a couple of steps. Brad had not stirred.

He said sharply: "Come *on*, Brad."

Brad followed Simon reluctantly. It was an easy walk to the mouth of the river, and they continued on inland to the grove of trees. There, having found a good place for spending the night under one of the bigger trees, Simon took the gourds and replaced the tepid brackish water in them with fresh water from the river. He had left Brad sitting beneath the tree and found him in the same position when he returned. He drank from the gourd Simon offered him, but did not speak.

Simon said: "I feel a bit more ready to chew that lousy pemmican. The fish can wait till breakfast."

Brad put the gourd down in silence. Simon's earlier irritation came back, more strongly. The whole idea of pressing west had been Brad's. He himself would have been content to settle in any of half a dozen spots on the way, where the pickings had looked fair and the natives friendly. He thought of Bos, who by now would probably have gathered his grapes and made his wine from them. Bos had not been such a fool as to abandon a good situation on somebody else's whim.

All that had happened since—the hardships, thirst and near starvation, blistered feet when shoes wore out, sunburn and fever and treacherous Indians . . . all these had been consequences of pandering to Brad's obsession. He could have been in Tenochtitlan still with Bos, living a life of ease. He felt he had earned something better than silent brooding now the trek was over.

He was framing a cutting remark when Brad said suddenly: "I'm sorry about today."

Simon felt there was not a lot he could say to that, and waited. The dusk was thickening; a crescent moon hung in a patch of deep purple sky clear of foliage. A new moon, like the one the night they climbed the pyramid. How many moons ago was it—seven, eight? They had long since stopped keeping track of time.

Brad went on: "I know it's not rational. I think I even understand what it's about—partly, anyway—but it doesn't alter things. The fact is . . . when we left Britain behind us to cross the Atlantic, it was different for me. I was going home. Perhaps not really home, but home country. And it's not, of course: how could it be? But it kind of knocks me out, realizing it."

Simon said: "But at the beginning . . . when we were in Algonquian territory . . . that was nearer where you'd lived, surely? And you were all right there."

There was another silence, which Simon let run, before Brad said: "When my parents divorced, Dad went to live in California, as I told you. It's a long way from Vermont. I visited him there a couple of times. The summer before last would have been a third time, but Mom and Hank had just married and she wanted me to go with them to Europe. We agreed I would stay with Dad for Christmas. But when Christmas came, we were with Bos and Curtius, on our way to Rome.

"I guess it was homesickness that made me think of doing a Christopher Columbus in the first place. The fact of New England's being so different didn't bother me that much. It was California I was set on; that's why I kept pushing for it. I knew Dad wouldn't be there—wasn't anywhere in this world—but I thought if maybe I could find the patch of coastline where his house had been . . . Actually, I don't know what I thought. As I say, it wasn't rational."

Simon said: "The way you figured it, this is southern California. The spot you were aiming for is maybe three hundred miles north of here."

Brad nodded. "Sure."

"We can make the last bit easily, now we've reached the sea."

"No," Brad said. "It's no help. I don't want to see that patch of coastline now. It would make it worse, not better. It's something I should have realized sooner. I've been a complete fool."

Simon thought about his own spells of nostalgia. Those had lessened with the passing of time, but it had been different for him. He had been on his home ground, which had probably made the immediate shock of switching into this alternate world greater. For Brad it had been something happening on a vacation, thousands of miles from home. The basic reality had not sunk in. In one part of his mind there had always been hope of a way back. Until now.

"We should have stayed in Tenochtitlan," Brad said. "Lundiga was an excuse; I see that. I've dragged you here for no good reason. I'm sorry about that, too."

"Well, we're here," Simon said. "And not doing badly, really. Interesting-looking country, nice climate."

Brad didn't answer.

Simon said: "Do me a favour will you?"

"What?"

"Eat your pemmican. Wherever we go next, I don't want to have to carry you."

Brad forced a smile. "All right."

Brad was restless during the night. At one point Simon heard him get up, and he was missing for about an hour. In the morning he looked tired and subdued, though he did respond when Simon spoke to him. They dropped hooks in the river but without success, and resorted to pemmican again.

When they were through chewing, Simon said: "I don't fancy trying to cross the river at this point. It looks deep, and that's a strong current running out to sea. If we are heading north we'd better go upstream till we find a better place."

Brad stared broodingly at the water. He needed pushing. Simon said sharply: "Well, which is it to be? North or south?"

Brad turned away from the river. "It makes no difference. South, I guess."

This time they walked side by side, and Simon waffled on about a variety of subjects—prospects of game, the kind of Indians they might encounter, the weather. It was talk for the sake of talking—anything to stop Brad from brooding.

He was in a really deep fit of the blues, Simon thought, and it might take some time for him to snap out of it. Their having no particular objective in view, after all the concentration on California, didn't help. And what *should* they do now, for that matter? They could head back to Aztec lands, but even apart from the problem of Lundiga he doubted if that was right. It would be good to see Bos again, but it would be a retreat, an acknowledgement of failure. There could be no going back.

No, this was as good country as any. They would maybe find an Indian tribe that would accept them, and settle to an existence of hunting, fishing, and the rest. There were worse ways of living.

He realized he had fallen silent, and began talking: "We ought to have a better winter here. Remember that snow. I'll be happy never to see a snowflake again. Do you . . . ?"

Brad had stopped abruptly. Simon wondered if he had changed his mind, and decided he'd rather head north after all. But he wasn't looking back. Pointing west he said, in a tone of wonder: "I don't believe it."

Simon looked where he was pointing. They stood on a ridge, with perhaps a quarter of a mile of level ground between them and the ocean shore. It stood halfway across that stretch, rising out of the bushes which had grown round it. It was in a state of extreme disrepair; near the top sky could be seen through it. But the outline was unmistakable, and one thing was certain: it had not been built either by local Indians or Aztecs.

"A classical pagoda!" The dullness had gone from Brad's voice. "A pagoda—in southern California."

They gazed further out, at the empty waters of the Pacific. More than five thousand miles of emptiness; but at the end of that, China.

With a note of rising excitement, Brad said: "I wonder . . ."